My Life Ignited

An Autobiography

Michelle Rose Johnson

My Life Ignited

ISBN: 978-0-578-777115-3

"The most important thing you leave behind,
when you leave this world, is your story"

–M. Rose Johnson

Acknowledgments

Never getting to know my grandma, and missing the opportunity to hear her life stories prompted me to write this book for my grandkids. It began as a story of my fire service career and ended up becoming an emotional journey of life thus far. As in any life, there is the good, the bad, the ugly, and the beautiful. I hope they take what is beautiful, and I hope they will see even in the bad good can result.

I couldn't have completed this journey without the support and encouragement of my sweet husband who believes I can do anything; I am so much more because of you. And thank you to *all* my friends and family who love me, just as I am.

A special Heartfelt thanks to Willitte Herman, the attention to detail and meticulous reviews made my writing . . . well, readable! You are amazing Willi!

Bonnie Yates, the 'comma queen.' Your love and encouragement gave me the courage to "write the whole story." You've been the best cheerleader ever!

This Book Is Dedicated To

My mom: Your love of true crime books fostered a love in me for finding out the truth, and an admiration for the investigators who figured out what happened. Who knew I would someday be "one of those guys"?

To my partner, Charlie: Your curiosity and quest to be the best made me a better fire investigator.

To my husband: You provided support and love . . . always.

And most importantly, to my children, grandchildren, and great-grandchildren: You can do, be, and have anything you set your heart and mind to.

M. Rose Johnson, May 2019

Preface

How did you come to be in the fire service?

This is a question I have asked others at least a hundred times in my past 23 years of fire service. The answers were as varied as the people who gave them. Many times, it was fulfillment of a lifelong dream. For others, it was fateful happenstance, or a job opportunity that became a way of life.

I have come to believe the Creator led me to this service; there is no way I could have imagined or dreamed this story up for myself.

At the annual Leadership conference in Janzen Beach we watched in fascination as presenter Gordon Graham showed case after case of witness accounts of the same (staged) bank robbery.

What was so fascinating was that while they all agreed the bank had indeed been robbed by a man, each witness saw the details of the robbery and the man differently.

The reason for this phenomenon, he explained, is that we all have different life experiences and filter things different because of those experiences.

This is a work of nonfiction. The events contained herein are portrayed as I remember them, to the best of my ability, through the filter of my experience, and do not necessarily mirror the views and opinions of others involved.

Every attempt has been made to contact the people mentioned in this book for permission for the use of their names. Most of the events are public knowledge, and presented with great respect.

—M.Rose Johnson

Chapter 1

"The only good Indian, is a dead Indian."

– Gen. Philip Sheridan
at a conference with 50 Indian chiefs at Fort Cobb in the so-called Indian Territory (later, part of Oklahoma).

Although I didn't grow up on a 'formal' reservation, we had a "rez" just the same. It had all the same elements of poverty, alcoholism, drugs, suicide, depression, and violence. This would be what I remember after my grandmother left our family, passing away from cancer in 1965. I was just 4 years old.

I have precious few memories of my grandparents. A vision of a long ride in the back of an open truck, jumping out to open an old wooden gate, and of driving through a rocky creek bed to get to their place.

Located near a creek, it is a place that shines forever green in my mind: A place of beautiful live oaks, waving grass, and rolling hills with a small house with no indoor plumbing, no electricity, or running water, the sound of Grandpa's baseball games broadcast over the radio, and gathering watercress with my grandma. To me, their lives seemed slow and peaceful.

Eventually we would learn that the home where they lived stood in the path of progress. A new highway expansion was planned that would make travel easier for those traveling east from Sacramento, California to the destination tourist resort area of Lake Tahoe.

I was born in the small town located east of my grandma's home. Nestled in the foothills of the majestic Sierra Nevada mountains, it is called Placerville today, formerly known as "Hangtown." It earned the infamous name due to the overzealous use of hanging as an alleged means of justice. In 2008, it became more blatantly politically incorrect; there was a prominent replica of what looked like a black man hanging by a noose on display where the original hanging tree was located.

After California had become the 31st state in the Union, Hangtown was changed to Placerville. In 1854, the county seat was moved here, where it has remained for the last 150 years. *(www.historichwy49.com)*

As a young child, I didn't understand that my ancestors' history was changed forever on January 24, 1848, when James Marshall discovered gold in the South Fork of the American River. Fed by the Sierra Nevada mountain range, it winds through the hills 10 miles north of Placerville traveling 120 miles to the Sacramento River. The discovery of gold triggered a mass influx of some 80,000 immigrants.

By land and sea they converged on the area, inundating the land.

The Native people who had lived there perished in great numbers. They died from starvation, disease, abuse, or were massacred. Their society, habitat, infrastructure, and culture were utterly destroyed.

This gold discovery spot is now noted as "one of the most significant historic sites in the nation." Located in Coloma California. It was designated an historic site to protect the remnants of the mill and town.

For many years afterwards, there was not much mentioned about the fact that Native people had lived for thousands of years in peace and harmony with their aboriginal land and environment. *(www.coloma.com/california-gold-discovery/history/)*

It is my personal understanding that when you take away a people's beliefs, customs, ceremonies, way of life, and dignity, it has a long-term negative effect. The result that I experienced was poverty, living on the edge, and reliance on government commodities. It became a way of life for many of the Native people who struggled with acculturation and assimilation.

In 1968 on a field trip with my grade school, we were learning the "history" of the area. What is burned in my memory was seeing an old yellowed newspaper ad tacked to the wall in a gold mining exhibit. The ad offered to pay 5 dollars for the head of an Indian. At the time as a kid, I was just trying to be okay with being Native, of looking too dark, somehow tainted, feeling inferior, and less than my white counterparts. Less pretty, less smart less privileged.

Many of the hardy descendants and survivors of these First Peoples have sought to rediscover and revive our heritage and culture. The political fight to gain back the recognition of the tribes that were originally located there still continues to this day.

Although things have considerably changed over the years, you can visit a small museum in the town of Coloma that is dedicated to sharing correct information about some of the indigenous people who were here before the gold discovery.

There are identified and protected grinding rocks located within the park. These are the rocks my ancestors used to grind acorns on. You can watch a short video featuring stories and memories of these indigenous people known as Miwok. You will see my mother and granddaughter among some of them.

At four years old, I was one of five children living at home. I was second from the youngest. Life was chaotic with motorcycle parties, drinking, and being home left in the care of my oldest sister, a whole 14 years old at the time.

I knew my biological dad. He took care of me before I can remember, taking me into a bar and having nice ladies change me when I soiled my diaper. He would take me to visit his family in Sacramento periodically. I always knew he loved me, he just wasn't around that much. Memories of childhood visits were few and far between.

People can make such a difference in a child's life. A neighbor that takes time to show a child how to read, a nice lady that lets a child help take care of chickens, an elder sharing a love of rocks . . . a sister that takes care of you. These are the people that, to this day, I am thankful for.

Chapter 2

"Individuals do not meet by chance. They are necessary in the experiences of others . . ." —Edgar Cayce

I was seven when my mother married the man who became the hero of my young life. In what seemed like a dream come true to my 7-year-old mind, we now had a house! We had protection. A real house we owned with no landlord to hassle us for rent! We went to school every day; we had food and security. He was a hard-working, dedicated man who provided stability. He quickly became a role model for me.

We were lucky to have him. Not many men would take on the task of raising children who were not his own. My eldest sister fled the nest as soon as she possibly could. That left two pre-teen brothers, me turning eight, and my youngest sister, a sweet 4-year-old. Not only did my stepdad take us all on, he and my mother would go on to have another son.

Studies show that children that are not loved and nurtured as small children will often act out in later years. Very often for girls, it manifests as promiscuity, looking for love in all the wrong places. Although we now had the stability my stepdad brought, the lack of love and low self-opinion I had for myself began to manifest as I hit my teen years.

My mother was in charge of us, 'her children,' and she did not know how, or have the ability to discipline. Inconsistency, threats, and an attitude of meanness accompanied any trouble. Whippings, which always failed, only made things worse. I began to spin out of control.

My mother was much better than before, however, now working at being a wife and mother. Her drinking was confined to weekends for the most part. But when she drank, I would do anything to avoid her. She threatened to send me away to an Indian school. In her day, this was a horrible fate. To me, it sounded good. I wanted to be sent away, so I kept getting in trouble. Something needed to happen.

Too many bad memories of long nights, bad choices, and the past, pre-step dad, stayed close to the surface. My mother did not, or could not help me as I floundered. Any important issues were only broached when she had been drinking, and in this I would not participate.

Uninformed and lacking any support for the most basic knowledge, I found myself pregnant at 15. Well, at least I *thought* I was pregnant. I didn't know! The basics of menstruation weren't even explained, so when the time came, I had to figure it out on my own.

Pregnancy certainly wasn't on the table to be discussed. Alone in figuring this out, I had crazy thoughts, "What if I hurt myself; if I fell off the roof the doctor would surely tell them, wouldn't he?" It would finally come out as I grew larger and larger wondering, "My god! am I going to have this baby by myself? What is going to happen?" I felt completely alone, there was no one to confide in. Nearing my eighth month, it could no longer be denied.

I remember distinctly the walk of shame, being escorted down the high school halls, the snickers of the high-class girls as I left the high school a pregnant dropout at the age of 15. Just another dumb Indian.

In the wake of this revelation there was not a lot of planning or conversation, although my mom did ask if I wanted to marry the father. "Marry! He's just a kid!" was my immediate, horrified reply. I was wide-eyed, going along waiting to see what would happen. I only remember feeling terrible, disappointing my stepdad, and happy that now I would have someone to love, someone to love *me*.

Once the truth was out, I let my pants out and ate to my heart's content. I wasn't alone, I was eating for two after all! The estimated due date quickly approached. Still woefully uninformed, I did not know what to expect at all. That day I was restless and more busy than usual. That night I tried to sleep, but could not. I was huge by then and being uncomfortable was the norm.

I finally got up, going into the living room where my older brother was who was visiting and watching television. After seeing my discomfort, he stated flatly, "You're in labor." What? Really? He had taken Lamaze classes with the birth of his son. He timed my pains, "You better get mom up."

My mom sat with me at the birth of my son. She soothed my brow and said lots of nice things to help me through the pain. I appreciated she was there, that someone was there. I always felt so alone. I wish she would have prepared me.

It was quite a shock, the whole birthing experience. I was so young and naïve, I had only brought a pair of Levi's and a cute shirt to the hospital, because I actually thought I would wear them home!

After what seemed a forever of pain, embarrassing procedures, and birth itself, I had a most beautiful boy with a head of thick dark hair. I thought, "Thank god, I can sleep on my stomach!"

His father came to see him. He was awed, though already in another relationship, he wanted to be involved. His mother and sisters would help.

Mom pretty much took over at home. She said I would not be breast feeding: I never asked why. I was so young I didn't question any of the decisions made. I did admire that my mom and family stuck up for me, as disparaging remarks were made. It was decided I would go to an alternative school. I started blowing it right away.

With my mom taking over care of the baby, I went back to being an out of control teenager. Soon I was banished from the house. Until I got myself together, I was not welcome to stay. I found myself floundering alone once again.

My brother and his wife tried to help. That soon ended when we went out drinking and his wife had enough of me. I was regulated to visiting my sweet son, which tore my heart out. I was on a self-destructive path, hating myself for being, for being me. The negative influences in the earlier years of my life had set this path for self-destruction. As I bottomed out, an unlikely savior helped me up.

Chapter 3

I like smoke and lightning
Heavy metal thunder
Racin' with the wind
And the feelin' that I'm under
–"Born to Be Wild," Steppenwolf

Crazy is how people would describe him: Biker, dangerous, party animal, bad news. Ben was 24 to my then just-turned sweet 16, and he was, or had been, all those things–by choice. He was also caring, kind, and loving to me. Deep-voiced, crazy, and dangerous . . . I liked him. He had a way of reading people, calling things as he saw them.

After listening to me cry about my son and watching me self-destructing, he sat me down. "You need help." Ben was not a knight in shining armor, but for some reason he loved me and wanted to help me.

And he did. My mom had said, "Get it together and you can have your son." Once I accepted his help, we got to work getting it together.

Our "getting it together" looked like a friend got him a job and let us move in with him and his wife. Ex-Gladiator biker and self-proclaimed crazy Mexican, he himself had recently "settled down."

He and his woman, Teri, lived at the top of a steep, winding grade in the little town of Kelsey. They had a baby the same age as my son. Life became learning to be a grown up. I did what was expected of me to do and tried to assimilate to this new life. A little crazy, a little settled down, Ben went to work, and I hung out with the Mexican's woman and missed my son.

Within a few weeks Ben said, "Okay, go get the baby today." Oh, Oh! Okay! Nervous, scared, and excited, my new friend, Teri, her baby, and I converged on my mom's house. She chatted with mom as I scooped baby chair, clothes, and baby; she didn't even have time to react. We were out of there! I had my son back. Eight months old, he was my buddy, mine to love and take care of.

It was a time of learning how to take care of a man and a baby. I felt I had never really known love, but I was learning. There was still partying. However, not to the level these guys used to party. It was all new to me. I was never good at it. Now that I had my son and was much younger than the rest of the crowd, I stayed home. Ben, however, stopped at the bars after work while I did the best I could to be a grown-up, married woman.

We finally got our own place and were happy in a little trailer; Ben worked, and I took care of my son. However, drinking was always an issue. Drunk driving arrests were almost a norm. Being so young, I was not very good at taking my birth control, "Oops, missed a day, oh I'll take two today" didn't work out so well.

Living in the small town of Garden Valley, we were far from town. Sick and not knowing why, I finally saw the doctor. I found out I was suffering from a terrible kidney infection, and I was pregnant.

I was happy, he was dismayed. Raising my son as his own was above and beyond anything he ever contemplated. He knew what he was getting into but, another kid in diapers? This was not in the plan.

This may not have been planned, but this baby was our love child. He would fall in love with her on sight. She would be born the day he was released from jail.

The night he was arrested began like many others. I was home with baby Bear, and Ben was out with my cousins drinking. When he came in at midnight wanting to go join them in Sacramento, my thought was, "I'll talk him into letting me drive." I was too young and inexperienced, but this is how I thought to keep our family safe.

I tried pleading with him, demanding he let me drive. We have babies to think about! In his drunkenness and stubbornness, he would not yield. I was too young, ignorant, and stupid to figure out how to avert the situation. The scary ride ended with the car flung across the intersection, head-on into a light pole.

We had run the light and been broadsided. As I came to, my first thought was, "Oh my god, what about the babies!" We broke the window to get out as the sirens screamed in the distance.

In the back of the ambulance, crying in fear, Bear and I were examined. Miraculously, the only damage was my broken foot bones and Bear's torn pajamas. He had just learned to walk and would have to relearn. The soreness of the impact bruised him head to foot. Ben was unhurt and taken to jail.

Full of remorse, but not really remembering the event, he was charged with drunk driving and ultimately would be gone for months.

I moved my friend, Tammy, in so I would not be totally alone. What a pair we made. Tammy with long, beautiful, wheat-colored hair stood 3'5", born with a condition called dwarfism, and me a ripe 17-year-old hugely pregnant. She was a good friend and anchor during a lonely time.

All this time I had relied on Ben. He drove us wherever we needed to go, and in classic denial did not think to prepare me for when he would not be there.

Now I would have to take care of us. Tammy didn't drive nor did I, which was a challenge. Tammy didn't have a car or license. We lived far down in the canyon with doctor appointments and family far away. I would need to step up; why hadn't we planned for this!

My only real experiences driving was with my two different fathers. Dad One let me drive once. The lesson came to an immediate halt when I sprayed rocks pulling out of the drive. Dad One was very particular about his vehicles and their care.

The second event was when I visited with my bio dad while he was in town visiting his family in Sacramento. This lesson started in a pear orchard. I was doing okay until I ripped the side mirror off on a low hanging branch. Oh crud, I thought as he jumped out. Guess my lesson is over. No, to my surprise he just threw the mirror in, and we resumed our driving.

Dad Two was completely laid back. His own learning experience driving had been when he bought his first car. He didn't know how to drive, so he talked the salesman into getting him out of town where he took over, white-knuckled, putting his cigarette out on the dash so as to keep his eyes on the road.

I would learn to navigate town and city by trial and error. I had to drive from pure necessity. Our old Indian car demanded transmission fluid every stop. I would jump out, huge, being pregnant, with a large, old wine bottle full of dark red transmission fluid, pop the hood, and give it a drink, no matter where we were.

As time went on, I struggled to keep it together to support Ben and prepare for a new baby. The day before Ben's release I was a ball of nervous energy.

Holding my hands to my back after hauling everything out of the trunk to clean the car, my friend remarked, "You're going to make yourself have that baby doing that." She was right.

Having been locked up all this time, Ben was thirsty upon his release. We went to a house of a fellow inmate he had met. As they partied it up, I sat thinking this is not how I envisioned this reunion, and my back hurts.

We arrived home, the special food I had prepared sat as Ben passed out on the couch. The pain I was in was intense. Trying to be positive, realizing I really was in labor, my thought was, I'll let him sleep a bit, then wake him for the ride to the hospital.

When I couldn't stand the pain any more, I tried to wake him. No go, he was out. I got my things together to drive myself only to find that wouldn't work. With every contraction, my right gas pedal leg would shoot straight out! He had to wake up.

After a scary winding drive to the hospital, I was taken to a room. The nurse turned to get a gown, hey, the baby is coming! In less than 10 minutes and with no doctor in attendance, I had my baby girl. Ben had found a gurney, curled up with baby Bear, and was going back to sleep when they said, sir, you have a daughter. He sobered up pretty quickly after that.

We examined the beautiful bundle of dark hair, perky nose, and intelligent eyes, what would we name her? We thought she was going to be a boy! After looking through a book of names, she became Teresa Marie. Sleepy-eyed, her 20-month elder brother thought she was a kitten.

Chapter 4

Do the best you can until you know better. Then when you know better, do better." –Maya Angelou

We did the best we could making lots of mistakes along the way. Despite the drinking, I clung to Ben. He was the only one who loved me for me. At his core, he was good and I saw that. Having suffered his own dysfunction as a child and having a biker vision, our life bordered on the wilder side with more arrests and jail time.

I had a beautiful daughter and a son. At 18 years old, I had my hands full. Still not mature enough to be consistent with birth control, I got my tubes tied.

Over the years, I came close to leaving the drinking that came with the life I was living, wanting more from life. But what would I do and where would I go?

We accepted aid, stood in line for commodities, and lived in the cheapest housing we could find. Always I "put up with" and "made the best of." Our family legacy was to be my norm.

Even as a too young mother without many prospects, I did have dreams. Vague and underdeveloped, they lay buried as I did what others expected of me with no questions asked. I accepted the position of a poor, uneducated woman that required aid to survive as the way it was, the way it would be for me.

Up until this point I had no vision for my life. I had been living the life that came to me: Surviving, but not thriving. Putting up with a life I was not that happy with. Letting others dictate my future, never considering that I might be able to design it for myself.

I had always been an avid reader. Searching for anything to read as a youngster, I pilfered from my mom's hidden stash and read true crime, illicit true love stories, even Steinbeck's *Grapes of Wrath* before I could understand it. The crime solvers fascinated me; they were cool! These were the guys who solved the case, figured out what happened, and brought the bad guys to justice.

As I grew older, what I was really drawn to were titles promising wisdom, knowledge, and destiny. I had always been, I realize now, a searcher. I started devouring self-help books. I was drawn to Maxwell Maltz ideas that we can create our reality. Edgar Cayce's life resonated with me. I had always felt I had lived before. I had no conscious memory of anyone telling me about reincarnation, but I believed in it. What did it all mean?

I searched for answers and wondered, was this all there was to my life? I still felt guilty and less than, even as a mother. I got to raise my son, but did I do him justice? Was I doing the best for my kids? I wondered about a word I heard a lot, Karma. What was Karma?

The answer to that question came after a conversation with a friend; we dubbed her "Debye White Van." Why, because that was the Indian name, we gave her. Deb said, "You need to meet Verna; she will do your numbers; she's psychic."

Deb explained she was hard to track down, so I was excited one day when Deb stopped in, "Let's go. I heard Verna's in town." Arriving at her house, her daughter let us in. She informed us that her mom would return soon.

After some time, the door flew open. She blew in the living room like a whirling dervish. Full of energy and light, she was happy to meet us and gave everyone a big hug. I liked her instantly.

Deb asked if she would look at my chart. Verna explained to me briefly that numerology was the study of numbers and cycles handed down from the greatest mathematician of our time. After carefully writing my full name and birthdate, they sat, heads together, eyes looking over a big book with the word "Numerology" on it. I wondered what they were seeing.

All at once Verna jumped to her feet, "Oh, my, I have to go." A whirlwind in motion she gathered things up. "Uh, what about my numbers?" She stopped at the door and looked me in the eyes. "You have a beautiful white aura. Stop wearing so much black!" (I was into the black leather, biker chick look).

Verna continued, "You are entering a year of hard work; hard work is as hard as you make it." Then she made a big deal of presenting me with a small, gold unicorn pin, making sure I understood this was *not* what she was giving me . . . huh?!

I left confused and a little fearful. Hard year? Yikes! Wasn't my life hard enough? I found myself the next day at my favorite place, the library. Later, with books about Pythagoras and his ideas of numbers in all things spread across my table, I could clearly hear and see Verna in my mind's eye.

All at once it was clear why she was laughing. What she had given me, the seeker, was my own quest in the longing for answers. It turned into a lifelong love of the study of Numerology and numbers in all things.

I began to research destiny and Karma, among many insightful things, but I was still floundering in my life. Dealing with dysfunction, I was searching for direction, and the wisdom of numbers helped. It got me thinking about what I came into this world to do. My numbers said a lot of things that I wasn't seeing. What could I be doing; what should I be doing?

Chapter 5

Learning is the beginning of wealth.
Learning is the beginning of health.
Learning is the beginning of spirituality.
Searching and learning is where the miracle process all begins.

–Jim Rohn

Good questions attract good answers and direction. Wisdom was coming my way. A big dose came to me through our local Indian Education Program.

We had people in our community who worked to provide services to Native people. Grant monies were obtained, the community benefited by way of a dentistry program, a health center offering classes for pregnancy, co-dependency, drug addiction, and cultural classes for the kids. It was designed to provide a sense of pride in the people, and a way to reconnect with our lost culture.

A wonderful relative I would come to know much better, Florence, was instrumental in gathering the kids to learn traditional Miwok dances. These programs allowed us to connect with what had been taken away and frowned on in the past. It would be one of the programs that led me to see a better future for myself. In fact, I would find the vision that would change my life.

The early 90's was some of the hardest, saddest times in my life. Not yet 30, with a son almost 15 spinning out of control, I realized I didn't know what I was doing! How does the child of a child develop self-discipline and become a young man without good solid guidance? The weight of failure to provide what he needed was on my shoulders. This was my fault, and the guilt consumed me.

It was this Indian program that would save me, save me from complete despair as I tried to deal with my co-dependent relationship and feelings of failure as a mother. Not only did I gain some self-discipline for myself, conquering a cigarette smoking habit though a Native stop smoking/wellness program, I learned about better living though healthful eating and taking care of myself.

Our instructor, Anita, explained this included taking care of our mental health, as well. It was Anita that steered me into one-on-one therapy. I would have never considered going to a shrink; I wasn't crazy! But I was so miserable I took her advice and made an appointment.

This lady changed my life. She didn't *tell* me anything, she asked a lot of good questions – questions I had never asked myself. What did I want *really*? And when I didn't know, pointing out the fact that I didn't have to know exactly. Looking at what I *didn't* want could be a clue! At one point, we did a hypnotherapy session.

After breathing exercises, in a very relaxed state, she asked me to remember a time that I had made a decision about love. I was instantly transported in my mind to a time when I was two or three years old. I could see this time so clearly! I was in my dad's truck, I looked at him attempting to get his key into the ignition, he was drunk and having a hard time.

I looked to my right, at the door handle. I thought, this is not safe! I need to get out. Then I looked back, but that's my dad . . . if I love him, I *have* to stay here. A snapshot of a decision, made at a time I could not consciously remember, had shaped my life! As a small child, I had decided that if you love someone you just put up with–whatever–even if that meant putting yourself in danger. Boy, hadn't that scenario played itself out in my life!

That clear realization changed my life forever. I had been living with a little-girl mentality about loyalty. It had led me to put up with what I did not want in my life. I walked away from that session with a different perspective. I left that session a different person as this realization washed over me: I did not have to put up with what I did not like! I could be in charge of my life! In my life thus far, I had always felt less than. Never finishing high school, I was sure everyone knew things I didn't.

I had eventually earned my GED through the Native assistance program, but I wanted more. I hated alcohol, and I had put up with it in my life for far too long out of a sense of, "if you love someone" you put up with bad behavior. I did not like being poor, I wanted a better life for my kids!

I wanted to be a good role model for my daughter. All I was modeling for her was smile, put up with less than you deserve, and like it! This had to end immediately. My therapist would help me see I needed to formulate a life plan.

I clearly remember the next day, sharing my life-changing revelation with my circle of friends. They were used to me "going along and getting along." They didn't laugh out loud, but their skepticism was apparent. That is never going to happen! Ben will not stand for an ultimatum. They were used to my codependent life style, too.

Change did not come easy, but I was determined. I decided I would move. I wanted to move to Oregon, and come hell or high water, I would do it! I knew a few things; I would never again live on assistance, and I would never put up with the dysfunction I had up to this point modeled for my kids. I would be in charge.

It was the hardest thing I had ever done, and scary standing up for myself and my vision of what life should be. It took every bit of courage I had. Telling the father of my children and partner of almost 15 years that he could come if he chose to change, or he could stay behind. Either way, I was leaving. For the part of me that always wanted to go along and get along, this was a major step. It was liberating.

With help, I made my plan of departure and set a date. It was an exhilarating time, but it was also a heart-breaking time. By then, my son, Bear, was repeating a family cycle of trouble. He would be spending time in a boy's detention center. I knew it was a testimony of his raising and a failure on my part as a parent. I couldn't change the past, but I could create a better future.

Planning was a big part of my success. I spent time visualizing myself being and doing a different me. It made me a different me. I would not jump and run away; I would do this right. I researched, I saved. We spent time with friends and family. I threw a huge going away party to say good-bye. Ben would stay in a state of disbelief up to the end.

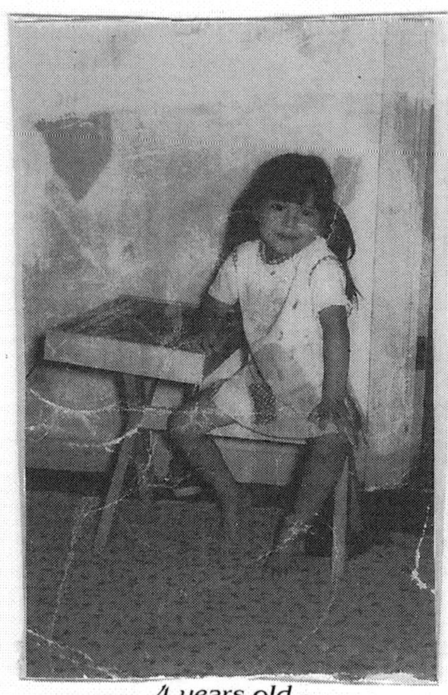

4 years old –
I always loved the idea of school

Mom and Dad.
My hero – The day they married our lives changed.

Grandparents Mamie and Clarence Padilla – I wish I could have known them better

My Dad Joseph William Chavez
A young dad

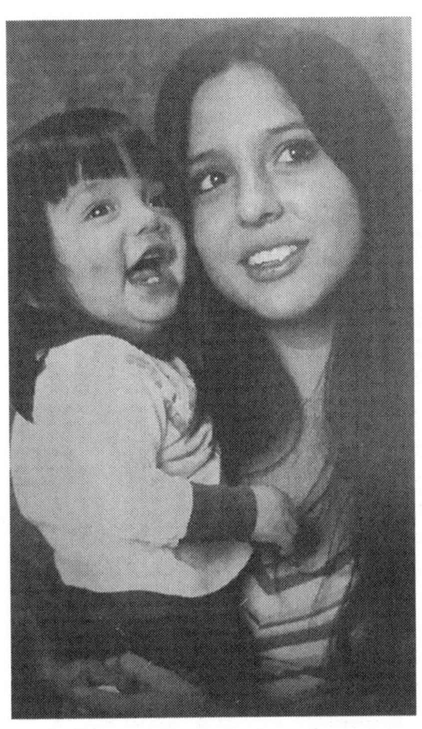

Teen mom – A kid myself

Family photo – good when it was good, trying to do our best

Hangtown – Placerville, California. Originally Indian Country

Ben Man – Sweet heart, bad boy, savior, and my love of 33 years

From parts and pieces in a box to this beauty – the 1977 Sportster Ben Man built for me.

Chapter 6

There is a road, no simple highway
Between the dawn and the dark of night
And if you go no one may follow
That path is for your steps alone

–"Ripple," The Grateful Dead

On a hot day in August of 1992, we left our little home town to start a new life. We left together, but the foundation was shaky. I didn't know if our relationship would make it, but I knew I would make this work. I didn't know exactly what I wanted. I just knew I wanted *better*–a better way of life for my children, I wanted to be a better me. I had hopes, but I really had no idea what I was in for.

=In past years, we had come to Southern Oregon to visit. My brother lived in the small town of Gold Hill, population 1000. We loved the little town, and we fell in love with the Rogue Valley. It was during one visit that we stopped by the bridge at Rock Creek beside the beautiful Rogue River just north of Gold Hill.

Gazing at the river and the lush green orchards, we vowed someday we would live here, too. Now here we were several years later, me with my vision.

My brother graciously agreed we could stay with him to get started. Located in the green shade trees above the water with an awesome deck, his trailer sat almost directly across the river where we had stopped on our visit all those years earlier.

The day was hot and smoky when we arrived. It was, as I would soon come to understand well, the peak of fire season in Southern Oregon. We watched as the fire known as Tin Pan Peak Fire belched smoke across the river from our new residence, wondering if our first experience in Oregon was going to be a lesson in fire evacuation! Soon the fire was contained, and we breathed a sigh of relief.

The next day, I drove myself to the local college campus. Sitting in the parking lot, I 'saw' myself attending this school. I was convinced that I was creating my life, that I was in charge. Now what would I create?

As I visualized myself attending school here, the negative voice we all have within tried to discourage me. How are you going to that? For what? I did not have a clue. I just kept saying to myself, I can do this, I will do this, the Creator will show me a way. I had no idea then that soon I would be attending classes here, learning skills in a field I had never before considered.

We unpacked and settled in. One of my goals in this new life was to do some things I had been too afraid to do in the past. I loved to sing, but I was shy. I decided I would get over that. I needed to tune my guitar! I didn't know how. In the past, my cousin Brian would stop at my house, play it, and get it back in tune. Now I was in Oregon far away from Brian and his tuning skills.

The little Yamaha had come to me on my eighteenth birthday. One of the nicest birthdays of my life, and the biggest surprise in my life ever. On that day when I arrived at my mom's house, I was presented with a gorgeous lavender and roses, heart-shaped cake. Ben knew I loved hearts, and he had it made by his sister, especially for me.

That was followed by the Yamaha surprise. When my brother walked in and set down a guitar, I thought my uncle was there. It took some convincing that this was for me, that my mom had bought me a guitar! I had always loved to sing. I knew all the old 60's songs verbatim. I couldn't believe this was my own guitar.

Some of the best times in my young memory was when my uncle and sister would show up to the house together. I would eagerly look to see if they had their guitars with them. Friends and neighbors would gather as my sister would belt out "*Kalijia.*" Our family had a history of musicians.

My only clear recollections were those times in our front yard and when uncle used to play at the tavern near their homeplace located out Highway 49 in Nashville, California. My mom had her Martin and shared memories of Grandpa playing mandolin and fiddle back in the day when my grandma was still alive.

That little Yamaha became a friend and a solace. Lacking confidence, I didn't know how to play more than

"*Bobbie McGee*" for years, but longed to play like my uncle and sister. Now in Oregon, I resolved to practice and get over my shyness.

My brother's ex, Judy, was a part of the Gold Hill Fire Department. She said, "I know someone who can tune your guitar!" Lesa Best was the lady who provided child care for most of the working mothers in Gold Hill.

Upon introduction, Lesa not only tuned my guitar, but became a lifelong friend. Energetic, fun, a piano and guitar player, Lesa and her husband, Glen, were active fire department volunteers. Lesa would be the one who would encourage me to attend my first fire department meeting.

The idea of helping others in a capacity that involved axes, big trucks, and the excitement of fighting fire . . . I may not have ever considered this before, but after the first meeting, I was hooked.

I joined immediately, eagerly awaiting the formal fire academy training that would allow me to be able to respond with the others on what I learned was not called a truck, but the fire *engine*. I immersed myself in this new culture. I wasn't ready to fight fires yet, but I was assisting with traffic control, cleaning hoses, learning the lingo, and the ins and outs of the fire station.

Finally, the day came. No more just hanging out and doing traffic control, I would soon be able to fight fire! It was March of 1993.

I stood, gear in hand, at the high school where our fire academy would be held for the next several weeks. I held my breath at the sight of a big red engine swinging into the lot, young men looking so professional as they set the chocks behind the tires that would secure the engine. *I want to do that!*

Academy was a grueling test–mentally and physically. Over and over we practiced donning our gear, identifying tools, gear, and protocols. After climbing down from the roof in full gear and breathing apparatus, I found myself gasping trying to pull in a breath of air, what the heck?! As I felt the suffocation, with no response from the rebreather, I realized my air had been shut off by the instructor! Better to simulate in training what to do if you find your air has been compromised, then in a fire where lives depend on you knowing what to do and acting quickly.

I gained confidence. Soon I had my certificate, and I was a firefighter and first aid responder. My family was proud and supportive.

We were a very small department serving a small community. Just over 1000 residents in an area less than one square mile. Founded in 1884, originally a settlement called Dardenells, Gold Hill was named for the gold discovered there in the late 1900's.

Our part-time paid chief, Bob Batte, was also the local minister. Every month he stood at the city council fighting for funds to keep up with mandated Oregon Occupational Health and Safety requirements, and creatively working with outdated equipment. Engine 7602, our second engine out, had to have the hood propped open to keep the engine cool when we went on a fire. We were a small but determined volunteer fire department.

Meanwhile, Ben, Teresa, and I were still living with my brother. After a shaky start, Ben had his own revelation about how he would choose to live. It had been just over a month living in Oregon when I arrived home to find him gone. I knew immediately he was drinking.

My old co-dependent reactions came up, should I go find him, keep him safe, pour him into bed? It was the wisdom of my daughter that brought me back to reality. We had been eagerly awaiting a program on television, seeing my hesitation she said gently, "mom Our show is about to come on" it brought to mind a saying, "keep doing things the way you always have, and you will get what you always have had". I realized this was not an occasion to turn back, only to sadly realize he was making his own life path decisions. The next morning as I left for work, I saw that he made it home.

When I called him from work, it was not with the anger of the past, just a sad confirmation that this was a choice, and we would be sad to see him go.

To my surprise, and after a lifetime of trying to force change for him, I came home to find a different person. This was a person who had a life-altering event. What had happened?

He explained that after our conversation, he went out and looked at his truck. He saw immediately that it was dented. He had been in some sort of accident. He had no idea what had happened–he could not remember. As he tried to recall the events of the night before, an Oregon state trooper pulled into the driveway.

In the short time it took the trooper to exit his patrol car and reach Ben, this life altering epiphany occurred. In a flash of realization, it occurred to him that he could be coming to tell him that he had killed someone, a child even.

The fact that he didn't know changed him in a way nothing had before. Was it the timing, my brother's sobriety, and the talks they had been having about living sober that this instance sunk in? I didn't know. I just knew he had been changed.

Knowing that my life had changed so quickly after my own epiphany, I recognized it was a true change. After a lifetime of drinking and being crazy, he quit cold turkey. My brother was a recovering alcoholic with some years of sobriety under his belt. As kids living in Placerville, they had partied and got into trouble together, now they went about being sober together. He would, in my opinion, become his best self in Oregon. I was happy and proud for him, for us.

We both found jobs with the same, small start-up company. Part house cleaning/part construction, I was thrilled we both were employed. My happiness soon turned to dismay at the lack of actual work.

I would use my gas to drive into town only to be told we had no houses to clean that day. My frustration was apparent. One day the owner, Glen, called me into his office to give me the "you need to go home and think about whether you really want to work here" speech. Go home? I didn't need to go home, I need to go to work, I need money!

I left there determined I would find a new job come hell or high water that day. I went all over town, I didn't have a lot of skills, but I had a lot of motivation. I went to one of Medford's largest corporations: Bear Creek. I didn't care that the sign said they were not hiring; I was desperate.

At the desk, the lady was on the phone having a conversation about a problem they were having with oversized amaryllis bulbs. It seemed it just came up they needed someone to peel them down to the right size to fit the Christmas boxes. I was their girl. I happily went back to tell Glen I had thought it over and . . . I quit!

At the dinner table that night, Ben told the story of how when he entered the office after work, Glen the owner said, "Your wife quit on me today!" My husband replied, "What did you do to piss her off?"

The job lasted long enough for me to conclude that if I was going to make it, I would need to do it myself. I sat down and made a plan . . . if I could manage and clean houses for Glen, why couldn't I own my own business?

I had cleaned houses in the past to raise money to leave California. I would need more practical experience and a mentor. After making signs and posting them everywhere, I got a call. Soon I was working for a fine lady, Carol. Carol had her own cleaning business. Working for her and learning from her helped me grow and gain information. I cleaned, and learned, and nannied part time.

Ultimately, I did start my own business called "Every Lil Thing," a business that supported me after Carol left to get married. I picked up her clients. This business supported my love of being a volunteer and the ability to craft my own schedule. My clients were supportive of my firefighting and would adjust cleaning dates when I had a big fire.

Before we left California, in preparation for our big move, my uncle, had let us stay our last days with him. He and I were watching the news when the story of a family in crisis was aired. He said, "You should help them, you're always wanting to help." Huh? I had never looked at myself that way, it is interesting what someone else can see in you that is oblivious to your own eye.

Chapter 7

Revvin' up your engine, Listen to her howlin' roar
Metal under tension Beggin' you to touch and go
Highway to the danger zone
Ride into the danger zone
–"Highway to the Danger Zone," Kenny Loggins

Now I was loving being a volunteer. Soaking up the culture, learning new things, meeting new people. The only downfall was that I was the last one to the station. Living out of town by the river, I would be last to arrive, and I would miss the engine and have to be on standby.

Standby was a secondary response. I could only respond once the engine left the bay, *if needed*. We soon rectified that situation when Lesa announced her neighbor was moving; we should get her house! It worked out perfectly. The first thing we did was put a gate between our houses for easy access.

Eventually we would buy this house, fulfilling a dream of owning our own home. Ben had a good job, never missed a day, and life was good.

Now, living right in town, many times I would be the first to arrive at the station. Often, I would get to take the driver's position as our captain rode shotgun. We trained every Tuesday night and attended many different classes.

Volunteers come in all shapes and sizes; one commonality is the dedication to be of assistance. As my life became one of response, missed dinners, and middle of the night emergencies, I found as my uncle had observed, that I loved helping.

It was fun, exciting, exhausting, and sometimes tedious, having to wait long hours in the middle of the night for a wrecker to clear the highway, or to get back to bed when I needed to work the next day.

I came to appreciate the heart of those who gave their time, energy, and heart to help others. This gift of assisting others is heartbreakingly apparent when the call involves the death of a child, failed resuscitation, or being a witness to the horror of an auto accident.

Training the mind to deal with tragedy, mangled bodies, sights, and smells that stay with you long after the call is over, is a challenge. Coping mechanisms must be found. Exercise and taking calls out with fellow responders help, but some calls never go away.

"7703 respond to Lampman Road." Approaching the scene, we were met with the sight of a pickup on its side where it had come to rest. It was obvious that speed was involved, this was a 20-mph corner.

What wasn't obvious was the body of a young man positioned flat under the cab. While the others involved were transported to the hospital, we sat with lights trained on the scene while we sat and waited for a large tow truck that would be able to lift the truck from his body.

Sitting in the engine, lights illuminating the scene, my mind reeled away from the fact that someone's someone was under that truck. Someone just lost their child, brother, friend–what was taking so long?! The minutes seemed like hours. Jumping out of the engine, I moved away to get that scene out of my head. I joined other responders standing on the other side of the engine talking.

Very quickly my mind refocused on school, how were classes going? Talking with the more experienced paramedics, I found myself laughing at a remark made. *Oh my god, did I just laugh?* I felt sick. How could I laugh when this boy is dead? How does the brain make sense of things that make no sense?

"7700 respond for a gunshot victim," I heard the dispatcher's voice from the living room as I dressed for work. As I raced out the door I thought, "Dang! It's early." Gunshots would be more typical after bar hours.

Our crew jumped in the rig and started out of town. The protocol for any shooting incident is for first responders to 'stage,' staying a short distance away to allow law enforcement to assess the situation and give an all clear.

The dispatcher was updating us as we pulled over before reaching the address. "This is two 9-year-old children home alone–the female has been shot–the male is awaiting response." Law enforcement was still 15 minutes out.

Lesa, Glen, and I looked into each other's eyes: we have kids. The thought of those children alone...we were not waiting. Entering the door, we were met with a hunched figure on the couch, face white with shock. Lesa immediately went to him giving him firm reassurance help was here. Glen and I raced to the bloodied bathroom.

His twin sister would die that day, a small 22-sized hole marring her beautiful forehead. A horrible accidental shooting, the event was a terrible shock to the victim's brother who was proudly showing her how he learned to hold his rifle. Home alone for a brief time waiting to catch the school bus, their world would never be the same. The community came together in grief, "*You Are My Sunshine*" was sung through tears for such a tremendously sad loss.

Today, you will see a sign just outside of the town of Gold Hill on Highway 234. The park was named for that beautiful girl, Alicia Fuller Park. It is an assurance that she will never be forgotten. No one who responded that day will ever forget her and the life cut short by a senseless accident. After calls like these, I would go home, smudge myself with sage, praying for understanding and for the family and the people affected.

Shortly after I joined the fire department, the City of Gold Hill voters supported a levy that allowed the fire department to purchase a brand-new fire engine.

What a privilege to drive that 1993 International brand spanking new engine! A Hale 1000-gallon pumper with a 1000-gpm monitor roof pump. It was something! Long, sleek, bright yellow for high visibility, it just barely fit into our truck bay. Backing it in, the mirrors cleared the bay opening by inches. Our chief had to specify that it could not be taller than 10 feet or longer than 30 feet. As it was, the bumper touched the rear of the bay.

When it came to responding during a mini blizzard in the middle of the night, snow swirling in the red and blue flash of our overhead emergency lights, we were immensely grateful to have an engine we could count on.

We had a new engine, but we still were operating on a shoestring budget. Small departments in Oregon overcome immense odds to provide emergency response to the communities they serve.

Regulations for training standards must be met, and equipment must meet strict requirements. Departmental needs are many, and our department was no different. At every city council meeting, our fire chief and captain would be in attendance rallying for our piece of the small budget to keep us going.

It was at this time that the city was approached by Jackson County Fire District 3 (hereafter FD3) with a proposal to annex the city into the district.

FD3 had purchased property at the edge of the city. Strategically situated near Interstate 5, it would house a new fire department in the future with or without the annexing of the city. After one year, we would vote to annex into the district.

FD3 was well established. Originating in 1951, a non-profit corporation named, "Central Point Rural Fire Protection District, Inc.," was formed to collect donations for creating a rural fire protection district. Central Point, Oregon, went from humble beginnings to one of the most progressive departments in the state. For us as volunteers, it felt like a rag to riches experience: new gear, leading edge training, up-to-date equipment, and a new station to house our engine!

Some fell away in the transition, some reveled in the change. Our part-time chief became a paid firefighter, and my bestie and fellow firefighter, Lesa, went to work in the office of the FD3 headquarters.

I immersed myself in all there was to know and learn: medical training, learning about and driving new apparatus, becoming involved with the volunteer association. Our training officer, nicknamed Bear, had a way of keeping you moving forward; it was a look and usually a short remark.

My fellow firefighters, Lesa and Glen, began training to become Firefighter 1 Certified. As volunteers, we were firefighter *academy* certified. That allowed us to be on the fireground and fight fire. I just wanted to help and fight fire, I didn't think I needed this certification.

The Firefighter 1 certification classes are designed to help a prospective candidate obtain a firefighter certificate for employment or as part of a 2-year fire science degree.

I went to the extra trainings tagging along to help them practice for the test. When the testing day came, our training officer cocked a brow and gave me a look, "Why aren't you taking the test?" You've practiced, you know this stuff, the look said, get your butt in gear.

Uh, can I? Not only could I take the test, I did just that and passed. That night at our annual banquet, I was proud to stand and be recognized with the rest of the class that earned their certification.

The next look came after a particularly bad medical call. A majority of calls in all six stations were medical in nature. "Why aren't you enrolled in the EMT program?" The emergency medical technician training is required to allow a responder to do more than CPR and give oxygen. After a lame answer of, "I don't know," I took these looks and remarks to heart. I pursued these certifications and skills, totally unaware of how it would benefit me in the future.

The classes were intense, engrossing, and fun! I was finally attending the college, just as I visualized that day. I would have never guessed this would be the subject.

Going back to school was intimidating and terrifying at times. Just the paperwork to get enrolled was overwhelming! Rogue Community College was blessed with an angel of a financial adviser, Brenda. Brenda always had a smile, loads of patience, and lots of encouragement. I still give thanks in my prayers for all her help.

Our classes were intense. So much to learn, all leading up to a comprehensive written test followed by a series of nerve-wracking, hands-on practical testing stations. Working and studying together, I would crack up to hear fellow classmate, Samantha aka "Ellie Mae," saying in response to any doubts, "Oh, piece of cake, can of corn!" Tall, strong and assured, Samantha would go on to become a paid firefighter with Medford Fire-Rescue, and in later years move up in the department. I was proud to know her and I loved her attitude. I adopted her mantra: "Piece of cake, can of corn!" After weeks of waiting, we would hear if we passed.

Soaking up new learning in class and now able to train with FD3, I began to get serious signing up to do "ride alongs" with the paid crew. Lesa and I would sign up at the Central Point station staying the night to run calls. We would spend time training with the paid crew driving the engines, learning about equipment, and going on as many calls as we could. We joined the on-duty crew, assisting and learning what the paid job of firefighting entailed.

On one of these overnight ride alongs, the call came over the radio: "7700 gunshot victim." Grabbing gear, 7731 shot out of the station, lights flashing. Bouncing in the rear as we made our way up a dirt drive, I tried to recall all the scenarios from the training in emergency medical technician class. Up until then, my training allowed me to do basic first aid, and I was looking at things differently as my skills expanded.

As we approached, the dispatcher warned that the scene was not secure. We would need to 'stage' the medical response rig until we got an all clear. Staging is when the fire department is responding to a dangerous situation that could put responders in jeopardy. Parking a safe distance away, we waited for law enforcement to get the situation secured.

"7731, responding to the scene," our driver responded to dispatch as we were cleared to come into the scene.

More bumps, red and blue lights illuminating the haze of dust floating in the air as we came to a stop.

Our patient was a male with a gunshot wound to his upper thigh. As our lead paramedic cut away the pants, I was amazed, it was exactly as our instructor described an entrance/exit wound would present. I observed a small caliber hole, relatively clean and neat. On the back side there was a fist-sized mutilated tissue exit wound. This was amazing stuff! "Training to respond and responding as you trained" was our mantra.

Chapter 8

"None of us, including me, ever do great things. But we can all do small things, with great love, and together we can do something wonderful."

–Mother Teresa

As I became immersed in my training, it was my personal mission being a female in a predominately male world that I would always conduct myself in such a way that I would earn my fellow firefighter's respect. My mission served me well. I didn't know it then, but much later I would instruct and train many of my fellow male firefighters, fire chiefs, and fire marshals.

At this time, there weren't a lot of women in the fire service. The first paid female firefighter in the United States was hired in 1973, yet women did not increase their numbers significantly until the 1980s. The 2000 Census reported approximately 11,000 paid female firefighters in the United States, roughly 3.7 percent of all paid firefighters in the country.

Interestingly enough, women have been firefighters for longer than most people realize, in fact, for almost 200 years. The first woman firefighter we know of was Molly Williams, who was a slave in

New York City and became a member of Oceanus Engine Company #11 in about 1815.

(Hollenbach http://digital.fireengineering.com/fireengineering/201404?pg=168#pg168)

During World War II, many women across the country stepped up to fill the void left from men gone to war. Many entered the volunteer fire service. Two military fire departments in Illinois were staffed entirely by women for part of the war.

There are certain criteria for any person in any given job. There is no one size fits all. There were now more female students in the fire science classes. It was easy to see the ones who were serious and the one who were there for male attention. The latter would fall by the wayside, while the serious would move up. From my own experience growing up with brothers, male cousins, and predominantly male friends, I liked and I could keep up with the give and take of firehouse living. The lively kidding and razing that goes with the territory of a testosterone-filled atmosphere was a mostly comfortable, fun challenge to me.

I requested to become an official 'sleeper.' The sleeper/intern program was designed for volunteer firefighters to gain "on the job" experience with a paid crew. I was assigned to our volunteer station at Gold Hill. After a brief period, I was assigned to our second busiest station located at our White City headquarters station with the paid crew.

Meanwhile, I was attending classes and working part-time during the day, and returning to the station to be on shift with my crew. The days we weren't on shift, I responded in Gold Hill.

The firehouse was built for men, but accommodations were made. I would use the small sleeping room the battalion chiefs used just off the main open sleeping area. Pulling my pillow over my head, I ignored the snoring that practically lifted the blanket from my body. I would eventually fall asleep, ready to jump up at the sound of the radio dispatch, happy to be a part of the team.

District 3 prided itself on being progressive and proactive. I was made to feel welcome. The younger guys seemed more open to change; as long as you could pull your weight, you were in. I found it was the older, "long timers" that were the most skeptical of a woman backing them up; she had to prove herself.

"7701 structure fire . . . " It was my first response with my shift. I was up and into my gear sitting in the engine adjusting my face piece when fellow firefighters clambered into the jump seat giving me an apprising look. The captain gave me a nod and thumbs up.

Constant training, pushing, more training, and testing assured me that I could and would be an asset to my team on the fire ground. The fighter agility test is a standard test for assessing important physical abilities for effective job performance. The tasks mirror real situations that firefighters encounter on the job. Consisting of eight "stations," this is a timed series, failure to complete the course in the allotted time was a disqualification.

Sucking air from the self-contained breathing apparatus on my back, I hefted the 45-lb hose pack and started up the first flight of stairs. Numbers marched through my mind, twenty-nine, thirty . . . a focal point of distraction, I occupied my mind as sweat collected in my mask, muscles screaming at the top, I made it.

Celebration of arrival at the top of the tower is short-lived, however. On to the next task, lowering the hose bundle hand over hand to the ground, just to haul it back up. Quickly I made my way back down the three flights of stairs to drag a 'charged' (full of water) hose 50' across the fire ground to the engine. Being vertically challenged, I had practiced time and again the best way to effectively maneuver the ladder off the truck and get it raised.

By far, the most challenging and important station for me was the dummy drag: Hauling a 150-lb "victim" after pushing my body to the limit. I had to prove to my captain and to myself that I could, and I would, be able to drag a victim or a fellow firefighter from a fire if need be.

As FD 3 volunteers, we were given the opportunity to excel. Running calls and gaining more experience grew my confidence. My emergency medical training made me an asset to our small community of Gold Hill. Now Gold Hill station responded with FD3 simultaneously, responding from Central Point with paramedics on board.

Before the district annexation, an emergency during the day might not have any response from our small department of daytime-working volunteers. I would hear the radio call from my job in Medford agonizing with those who were in trouble, feeling every long minute until a unit arrived to the scene.

The response they were waiting on would be from Mercy ambulance and FD3. This would typically be a 7-minute response. Long minutes stretch out into what seems like days for those awaiting help in emergency situations. In response to the needs of the city, FD3 would have a shift on site to cover our city, with a new station to be built in the near future.

The need for speed bred new protocols. The period of time following a trauma or injury during which there is the highest likelihood that prompt medical and surgical treatment will prevent death is called the Golden Hour. It was the goal.

While initially defined as an hour, the exact time period depends on the nature of the injury. Especially with a heart attack the chances of survival are greatest with quick response. Our new protocol would allow us the use of the latest technology. We received a new defibrillator for the Gold Hill station. Since I was now a certified emergency medical technician (EMT), it was in my scope of practice to use it.

Each level of training has a defined role. A first responder could give basic life support measures including oxygen use and first aid. But a certified EMT could provide more medical support, such as epinephrine for an allergic reaction, and a trained certified paramedic could give the highest level of care administering medications and advanced life support measures.

Although development of practical defibrillators began in the 1920's, a modern, compact, easy-to-use life-saving device in 1998 was a new tool for us in small town Gold Hill. In the near future, these devices would become so standard that today you can find them everywhere for public use; even school children are being taught how to use them!

"Engine 7703, respond to heart attack victim . . . " I was already clicking through the checklist in my head as I flew to the station. At the scene, I applied the leads to a male's chest and flipped on the machine. We had what we call a 'shockable rhythm,' the heart was in ventricular tachycardia, which is when the heart is beating abnormally, it is not pumping blood effectively to the rest of the body. This can deprive your organs and tissues of oxygen. After an "all clear," the machine made its peculiar wind-up sound, a shock was administered–we were successful! The ambulance arrived to whisk the patient to the hospital.

Around the turn of the 20th century, cardiac arrest became a leading cause of death. While inventors had touched on the idea of using electric shock to restart the heart or correct a heartbeat beginning in the late 1800s, heart surgery pioneer, Claude Beck, performed the first successful defibrillation in 1947 on a 14-year-old boy experiencing ventricular fibrillation during one of his surgeries.

Beck administered an alternating current of 60Hz to the

boy's heart and, on the second try, the heart successfully restarted. Thus, defibrillation was born.

https://healthtechmagazine.net/article/2017/08/defibrillator-jump-started-cardiac-arrest-survival

The external defibrillator, as it is known today, was invented by electrical engineer, William Kouwenhoven, in 1930. William studied the relationship between the electric shocks and its effects on the human heart when he was a student at Johns Hopkins University School of Engineering. His studies helped him to invent a device for external jumpstart of the heart.

Defibrillation by emergency medical technicians without the presence of physicians was first performed in Portland, Oregon, in 1969 (Joseph J. Bocka, MD, Attending Emergency Physician, OhioHealth MedCentral Health System; Emergency Medical Service Medical Director, Multiple EMS Service; Ohio EMS RPAB Region Chair).

Now they had a way to access and treat the heart's dysrhythmia without open heart surgery. This allowed what was now becoming a standard practice: emergency medical technicians reviving victims of heart failure in the field.

Now that I had achieved my goal of earning my emergency medical technician certification, our crew could cut down the waiting time and address the Golden Hour more efficiently.

Hours of training and grueling testing were all worth it. I wanted to be able to do more, I visualized helping many people.

The "more" of my training was demonstrated to me shortly after my certification. Sitting in our office at the station one afternoon, I heard a car screech to a halt outside the front door. A woman jumped out to help her friend as she collapsed to the ground beside the car, "She's been stung, she's allergic!"

Calling for help, I grabbed the kit and assessed her small sting marks and looked for any symptoms of anaphylactic shock. The effect of epinephrine is a beautiful thing to see. After administering the dose, she immediately sat up and felt better. It was just as the books described. The fact that the woman would have had to wait long minutes without my new training was not lost on me.

Chapter 9

"So she searches for light, only to realize it's in her, like an ember equipped to ignite."

– Jessica Sorensen

My love for fire investigation came while attending a 'hands on' course sponsored by our fire district. Our instructors would be deputies from the Office of the State Fire Marshal and Oregon State Police Arson Division. The team would instruct and set actual fires that we, the students, would investigate after the classroom portion of this event. It sounded like it would be good experience and maybe some fun.

As the day of classroom education proceeded, the cadre of instructors added more and more information explaining the techniques of layering. They explained the methodical process of examining blackened debris, looking for fire indicators, and "reading" a fire. I was amazed and awed by these men.

They painted the picture that we could trace the fire back to its origin by knowing how things burn, I was fascinated! It was at that precise moment that I thought, *"I want to be one of those guys!"* I was so impressed with the knowledge in the room. I sat enthralled with this new information.

The man sitting directly behind me obviously was not. This guy was being completely noisy and obnoxious. The elder deputy in attendance was a deputy state fire marshal named Ed Harris. It was Deputy Harris's turn to teach his portion of the class. The disrespectful man sitting behind me continued talking and making rude comments. I felt my temper rising as the instructor did everything a good instructor can do to deal with such a student.

I had just about had it with this guy when he nosily opened the newspaper and began to read! I spun around hissing, god knows what, I was so furious at his blatant disrespect of an elder. He glared hatefully at me as we broke for our lunch break.

As we left the room several of the guys gave me high fives. They were just as disgusted as I was with this guy's behavior. After lunch, Leroy, a six-foot-tall, strong-as-an-ox firefighter planted himself in the guy's chair, arms crossed. We were disappointed when he and his fellow partner did not return to class.

At our next break, I noticed a note stuck on my windshield. It was a hastily scribbled note that alluded to being a stupid woman, ignorant Indian out of line, and about the inability to pay attention. I passed the note along to our local deputy,

Wilbur Strait. He was not happy. It was at a special request of their boss that the instructors had made special provisions for these two police students to attend the class. Because of this incident Wilbur would remember me in the future when I looked to him for information and direction.

I soaked up the information taking copious notes. I spent the evening studying and imagining myself as a fire investigator, preparing for the next day when we would have our own fire scene to process. It was realistic alright! It was dirty, smelly, dangerous, black, and intimidating; I fell in love.

They had actually set fires in every room assigning students to work together to come to a conclusion as to how the fire started, what were the first items ignited, and how the fire spread. I was amazed.

I was to learn that in partnership with fire departments across Oregon, the Office of the State Fire Marshal provides the live-fire, hands-on, basic fire investigation courses. By law, the fire marshal is responsible to see that every fire is investigated in the state of Oregon.

This type of training is important because it provides local departments the ability to make causal determinations of fires when possible. If the local chief or investigators need assistance, a deputy state fire marshal will respond to conduct the fire's cause and origin. Unknown to me, in the future I would teach these classes.

The classes take time, energy, lots of resources, and cooperation. It is usually initiated by a fire department that would like to host training. The goal is to have realistic fire scenarios, a real fire scene for students to investigate. The ability to read fire growth and movement is about studying the structure, the contents, and visible remains after a fire occurs. We worked to make sure our 'house' was as complete as it could be. Goodwill Industries proved to be a good partner for obtaining these things.

The local department determines the class location, sets dates, plans logistics, and prints handouts provided by our office. The fire departments will work with the local deputy state fire marshal who will in turn find available deputies and arson detectives to provide the training.

The first day of class consists of a day of classroom learning and testing. Then the fun begins. Fire department personnel not attending the class gear up for suppression. The house, now fully furnished, is mapped out, with rooms marked and set up for fires to be set in individual rooms.

There is much consideration given to these fake "fire sets," ensuring that the students will have a meaningful, real investigation experience. The scenarios would include the leading causes of fires trending in Oregon.

Scenarios are crafted so that students use all that they have been taught. The scenarios are made to be as realistic as can be, with facilitators acting the part of home owners, responders, and witnesses for interviews. The scenarios have several potential causes within a fire room. Not only are students to report on what *did* start the fire and how, but a good investigator has to eliminate what *did not* cause the fire, and explain why.

In the careless-smoker scenario, there might be a

heater set close to the burned chair. Close examination and debris removal would reveal that the heater was not plugged in; therefore, it could not have started the fire.

This is the basis of the Scientific Method students are to learn; a method of ruling out potential ignition sources, examining and layering burned debris, hypothesizing causes, and finally determining a cause and origin.

The following day is the actual fire investigation. The students respond as if they were fire investigators called out for a real fire utilizing all that they have learned, photographing, diagramming the scene, interviewing, and examining the physical evidence.

The course concludes with the teams of investigators writing and giving their reports verbally. They will explain in detail how they came to their conclusions as to the origin and cause of the fire they investigated.

The final agony, and glory, comes after they state their final determination of origin and cause. At that point, the class views the videos of the fires each team investigated. Watching exactly how all the fires were set, from ignition to suppression, the effects of suppression and of items actually consumed in the fire, students could see if they interpreted the patterns and information correctly. It is humbling, informative, and educational.

After the investigation, class is concluded. The house prop will continue to be utilized as a fire training tool and provide live fire-training for new firefighters.

As a firefighter, these "burn to learn" activities provide a chance to understand the terms and witness situations first-hand that, up to then, were only described in books and lectures. It provides the chance to observe the unburned products of combustion and gases, ignite; the fire appears to be bubbling and "rolling over" at the ceiling level as they crouch below it with limited gear and a hose full of water. Feeling the intense heat, watching the smoke layer gathering at the ceiling and filling the room is the best training to prepare new firefighters for the real deal.

Attending that course changed my life. Up until then, I was just happy to serve, to help people, fight fire, and have a lot of fun doing it. I had never thought of actually making a career out of what I was doing.

After the class, I contacted Fire Marshal Deputy Strait, he remembered me, and agreed to meet. Over coffee, he filled me in on some of what it would take if I was serious about fire investigation. He explained I would need to join the local chapter of fire investigators in our area.

The International Association of Arson Investigators is an organization with more than 9,000 fire investigation professionals, with 70 chapters located all over the world. With a vision to "serve as the global resource for those working in and associated with the fire, arson, and explosion investigation profession with respect to fire safety and prevention; arson investigation, determination, and prosecution; and fire loss claims and litigation."

https://www.firearson.com/About-IAAI/Default.aspx

If I was serious, Deputy Strait would speak to my department about me then he would be willing to sponsor me to uphold the mission of our local state chapter 31.

After speaking with Deputy Strait, I made an appointment to talk with our Fire Marshal Lou Guggliotta. I liked Lou; he was for the most part, smiling and good humored, and as serious as a heart attack when engrossed in his work. He was easily identifiable with silver hair and a handlebar mustache to match. His wife, Betty, a skilled trauma nurse, had taught our burn section of our emergency medical technician class.

He listened carefully as I explained my goals, asking questions as to my reasoning. Ever progressive and supportive, FD3 endorsed me in becoming a member of the Association of Arson Investigators. Attending my first meeting, I was impressed by all the different representatives who had an interest in fire investigation at the table.

Included in the members were the deputy state fire marshal, local fire marshals, Oregon State Police arson detectives, insurance fraud investigators, and private fire investigators. At any given meeting, a guest might include a district attorney speaking on the necessary information to prosecute arsonists, or the medical examiner speaking on the telltale effects of death from fire.

Chapter 10

A thing ain't a thing until ***you*** *call it, and give it a name"*

—Ko Sensei Robert E. Walker -AKA "Toad"

Could I be a fire marshal? The idea danced around in my head. I finally found my way to the resource center at the local college. Finding the fire section, I was surprised to see that I could check off several of the boxes outlining the fire science degree requisites; I found things I had already accomplished on the list. My Firefighter 1 Certification was part of it, along with my emergency medical technician and fireground classes that I had already completed. I began to seriously consider that I could do this.

I had a talk with my training officer. I was ecstatic the district would support me in my goal to obtain more investigation experience. I had permission to assist with as many fire investigations that I could attend. I left that day with a letter signed by our chief.

With my letter of support, I visited all the local fire departments, meeting with the various chiefs and fire marshals. I interviewed the people who were doing investigations on a regular basis. I was requesting permission to learn from the best. I was approved to respond and assist with their fire investigations. This allowed me a unique experience to work with many excellent investigators, state police arson members, and get to know the ins and outs of the private investigators who show up on scene on behalf of insurance companies.

I went to every fire I could. When the pager went off, I would head out, contacting the lead investigator en route. I knew that when they got an investigation call, contacting me to assist was the last thing they would be thinking of.

During this time, I was working, volunteering, and going to school. I had established my own business which afforded me the flexibility to set my own schedule while going to school and responding to fires.

The clients I had were some of the most supportive folks. They worked with me changing schedules at the last minute if something big came up. I couldn't have accomplished all I was able to do without my family support and good client understanding.

At this point, I was devouring any and everything related to fire investigation and inspection. I was alert to any class, any opportunity that would grow my knowledge. I signed up to attend the Oregon Volunteer Firefighters Association Conference (OVFA). OVFA provides representation and support for emergency responders for volunteers from all over the state.

The Conference had an impressive schedule of the latest and greatest training for firefighters. My focus was on the fire investigation class being taught by the Office of the State Fire Marshal.

At the evening networking fundraiser, I found myself being introduced to the new local deputy state fire marshal (DSFM) for our area in Jackson County, Charles Chase. Deputy Chase had been recently hired to fill the DSFM position after our local deputy, Wilbur Strait, had suffered a massive heart attack and passed away.

I had attended Wilbur's service, which was held high atop a beautiful hill overlooking the city of Ashland. I arrived and stood looking back at the winding road leading to the site. The view of engines that lined up for a mile was impressive. I was awed by all the fire personnel in attendance looking sharp, respectfully dressed in their Class A uniforms. It would be my first experience of the bells, the bagpipes, and the bell ringing ceremony.

The Ringing of the Bell is a ceremonial announcement that a comrade has come home for the final time. A bell is run three times in sets of three. After each set of ringing the bell, the ringer, with a gloved hand, gently grabs the bell to silence it before sounding the next ring of three. At the final toll of the third pull, the bell is left alone to ring out. There are many different versions of how many times this is done based on different departments' traditions.

When the Irish and Scots immigrated to this country, they brought many traditions with them. The tradition of bagpipes played at fire department and police department funerals goes back over one hundred and fifty years in the United States. Hearing the mournful voice of the bagpipes playing, to this day, will make me tear up for all those for whom I have attended their last call.

At the OVFA conference, I learned that Deputy Chase would be the instructor at my up and coming investigation class held at Rogue Community College. In the future, I would become his shadow, and he would encourage me to apply at the DSFM's office when an opening came available.

I started a semester of cooperative work experience. It was a semester of internship earning college credits in one's field of study. I was able to spend that semester shadowing our Jackson County FD3 Deputy Fire Marshals Neal Shaw and Roy Brown.

Stationed at the White City headquarters, the two deputies were responsible, not only for fire investigations, but the many duties of fire inspections, plan reviews, fire planning, prevention education, and everything else pertaining to the Fire and Life Safety Division. They reported to our fire marshal who divided up the district for them to cover. I was amazed at the magnitude of what the Division accomplished. Up until now, I had only concerned myself with one aspect of our district's many functions: operations. It was eye-opening to experience the whole picture.

The semester ended, but my scheduled time continued. I was gaining valuable hands-on experience in codes and enforcement, fire prevention education, plan reviews, and best of all, fire investigation.

Thankfully, there were not more devastating fires. I was getting experience assisting with every fire I could, but I needed more hands-on experience. The chance to gain more experience showed up as a shadowing opportunity at Portland Fire & Rescue. "If you really want investigation experience, you should apply to do a ride-along with Portland Fire," the fire marshal from Cottage Grove encouraged me.

Portland Fire Department has a long, exciting history from the days of the "fire eaters," men who wore long mustaches held in their mouths to filter smoke from the fires they fought, to the horses who carried water to the fires. Portland was deemed "a city built to burn," comprising rickety warehouses, and miles of wooden docks soaked in petroleum.

In 1912, it became obvious it would be best to stop fires in the first place. A businessmen's group organized to promote fire prevention in the downtown district. J.W. Stevens was appointed Portland's first fire prevention officer (www.pdxhistory.com). The prevention and investigation division has since grown.

After gaining approval from the Portland fire marshal, I was accepted to ride along for one week. I reported to Old Town Station 1. I was a little apprehensive not knowing what kind of reception to expect. I was soon relieved of my nervousness as the crew and members of Station 1 warmly welcomed me for my scheduled week of "ride along."

It so happened that their female firefighter, Rose, was out of the station away on vacation. I would get her semi-private cot off the main sleeping bay. I was given a pager for response; I would be on call for any and all fires that the rotating fire investigators responded to.

The fire investigators worked shifts. It was a great opportunity to meet different investigators; I would get the buzz from my pager and hurry downstairs to the garage where I would meet up with the investigator on duty at that time.

I would spend this week working more fire scenes than I had previously worked in several months. The pager was regularly calling the investigator out. Off and running, we investigated a school fire, interviewing and getting a confession from two adolescents. I was surprised to find that Portland fire investigators are sworn officers. This is not typically the case with most fire marshals.

We responded at all hours of the day and night. I found myself surveying the city from atop a high-rise building where we determined a worker left before the required time (fire watch), resulting in a fire in the space where he was sweating pipes with a torch.

Next call, we determined hot ashes on the porch caused minor damage to the exterior of a home, and spent time tracking down and interviewing children when some garbage in an alley mysteriously ignited.

At 1 am, response to a car fire. Located in a remote area, it was found to be a stolen vehicle. The items inside ignited.

3 am, a call to the airport where I took photos of the unmistakable burn patterns of an ignitable liquid splashed on a vehicle. There were accidental fires, a chimney fire. It went on and on. For every fire I attended, I made notes in a small book. This documentation would prove very helpful to me in the future.

I learned a great deal from each of the capable investigators I responded with. I found myself treated to a grand tour of the workings of Portland Fire, and had the opportunity to see how such a large organization worked. The overwhelming daily requests for assistance, with not only fire investigations, but plans review, fire prevention, plus emergency calls all day long, was an eye opener.

I was impressed with the television station for making those great messages they broadcasted; there was a talk with the Chief and a forum for folks wanting more information. I found myself in some of the oldest buildings in Portland old basement rooms that echoed of times long passed.

Riding along on the engine responses on a night when investigations were slow was the most thrilling. Lights and sirens pulsing through the city, finding our way to the hurt, the sick, and the injured, it was like being in a movie . . . riding with the good guys.

It was an honor to meet all these fine folks. Not many get to experience the inner workings of such a large, progressive department from the inside out. It was an honor and a reflection of how departments work together in Oregon for the betterment of the people who live and work there. In the future I would come to know these investigators much better, attending fire conferences, courses, and classes together.

I returned to my district more confident and more determined than ever to be a great fire investigator and inspector. More and more, my experience and knowledge grew with every response.

Gold Hill volunteer

Lesa and I – my bestie driving big trucks and having a blast!

Gold Hill Fire Department

Fatal car fire investigation with Arson Detective Fields

(Portland fire) Riding with the "Good Guys"

(Graduation) First in my immediate family to go to college

Office of the State Fire Marshall

Incident Management Team on a Conflagration near Summer Lake Oregon

Early days, Deputy Chase and I would go on to investigate many more fires together.

Oregon Volunteer Firefighters Association – Investigation class Cadre (left to right) Deputies Chase, Mills, Warner, and Crosiar.

Oregon Fire Marshal Annual Meeting – A quick ascent to presidency

Rescue training, Serious fun! – Graves Creek, Oregon

Chapter 11

I can still feel the breeze that rustles through the trees
And misty memories of days gone by
We could never see tomorrow
No one said a word about the sorrow

–"How Can You Mend A Broken Heart," Bee Gees

"There's a baby in there . . . ." We were standing outside of a partially burned single-wide trailer. Looking into my eyes, Deputy Chase was attempting to prepare me for the first child fatality I would experience. How do you prepare your mind, your heart, to see a dead baby? Unsure of what to expect, sobered and serious, I braced myself to see a burned body.

I, like many others, expected a person who died in a fire to be extensively burned. I had only experienced a couple of fire deaths, and the bodies were involved directly with fire and burned so that my mind could classify it just as "the body."

This was much more intense, more intimate, more real. It was a shock to see what looked like an ivory, antique, porcelain doll. Perfectly preserved like a fine china doll, the child lay with eyes closed as if in sleep. With reverence and a sick heart, we gently brushed the debris away and took the required photos.

People don't typically die from direct fire. They die from inhalation of the toxic smoke. So many times, our prevention messages, "Check your smoke alarms," fell on deaf ears. Every year people die in fires in a home with no early warning alarm that could save their lives.

The mother of this baby would be air-lifted to the burn center in Portland. Suffering from burns to her body, the scars she would live with for the rest of her life would go much deeper than the third-degree burns she suffered.

The horror of her family and neighbors, as they tried in vain to rescue her and the baby, would most certainly be seared into their memories forever; scars of knowing a small child had access to a lighter while his mom and sibling napped, were perhaps even more deforming than physical burns.

Using a methodical approach, we began our investigation. After examining the fire, examining everything at the scene, from the least amount of damage to the most burned, we could determine the room of origin to be the living room. The extensive damage to the floor in the middle of the room was our area of origin.

In a fire investigation, the investigator will be identifying and documenting the patterns that identify how the fire grew and spread, working backward from least to most damaged.

We carefully continued to search for the point of origin. The point of origin is defined as the exact physical location within the area of origin where a heat source and the fuel interact, resulting in a fire or explosion. Typically, a fire in the middle of a room sets off warning bells, what is there to accidently ignite a fire in the middle of a living room floor?

For a fire to ignite accidentally, there must be an ignition source. Was there a heater there, faulty light fixture above, or faulty wiring below? The "dig" would tell the story.

In a blackened fire mess, it looks as if everything is destroyed, but what remains tells a story to the fire investigator. Examining the hole, we could see what is called a saddle burn, a descriptive fire pattern name to describe the charred edges of a hole burned into a surface. It indicates that the fire had burned down into the hole, a telltale sign that the fire came from above and had not burned up from under the floor into the structure.

FD3 Deputy Mark Moran shimmied under the trailer. Examining the underside, he confirmed there were no electrical wires in that area or ~~no~~ remains of a heater. But interestingly enough, in the remains of burned debris was a Bic-type lighter.

We would find lighters in and around the house. Only later, after we processed the scene would we learn that while mom and baby had been napping, the 5-year-old had been playing with the lighter. He ran out of the house when fire ignited.

A working smoke alarm to provide early warning to escape before the smoke is too intense could have saved a lot of heartache, not only for this family, but for those who responded as well. The web of a tragedy like this one spreads wide: the distress and agony of those neighbors and family who ran to help, the anxiety that a dispatcher feels, knowing for the caller that minutes seem like hours, the emotions of the off-duty fire official that stopped to help, but could not, will stay with them forever.

As fire investigators, we all have our nightmares. My friend and mentor, one of our two FD3 Deputy Fire Marshal's, had a fear of being in just such a horrific position as he found himself that day. He just happened to be traveling by when he saw the small trailer on fire. It was his nightmare come true. They take these horrific calls home after their shift. They take the feelings of hopelessness and sadness of the firefighters on the scene, who instead of rescuing, have to recover a body or bodies, which can be devastating.

The investigators who will assist with the body removal are capturing everything through a camera lens, imprinting devastating images; these are things that cannot be easily forgotten. It's the same for the medical examiner and assistant who will transfer the body and perform the autopsy to determine the actual cause of death. The district attorney who must be notified of a fatal fire incident, feels it. The media reporter, the people who will wake up to this tragic news event, they are affected too. Lastly, so too with the State Fire Marshal who will gather statistics, and sadly report yet another Oregonian lost their life in a fire.

As a firefighter, I never really questioned that these events were happening every year. I hadn't any real idea that we already had technology that could prevent people from dying in their homes. As a firefighter, we concentrated on putting the "wet stuff on the red stuff."

In June of 2000, my path continued in a positive way. I walked the stage with my fellow fire science class graduates, the only female in a class of 35. I was the first in my family to earn a college degree; it was a proud day for me. I sat in the hard-back chairs watching the crowd, thinking of the people that had encouraged me and believed in me. I would not be here without their support.

It is funny that someone else's view of you can change the way you see yourself. Not only did I have the support of my family, friends, and the district, I also had support from the clients that I cleaned for. I thought back to the day working at one of my favorite client's beautiful home. I noticed a book, "The Energy of Money," on the shelf as I dusted. Duane, can I borrow this book? Duane was a successful retired Volkswagen mogul; his house was located on the golf course in Medford. The title of this book interested me. Knowing what I did of Duane, I expected to find an analytical, serious read on finances.

I was surprised to find it was not. This book was very different. This book asked how you felt about money? What was your first experience with money growing up? How did you see money? It was my first introduction to the concept of vision boarding.

The book explained it was a method of attracting money. I was excited to read about what I already believed: we are always attracting and creating. The gist of the chapter on attraction was that you actually made a board about attracting money with pictures! It blew me away! This was more esoteric and what some might consider "woo woo." It was based on the concept that money is a form of energy.

I wouldn't completely understand this concept until much later when I attended a Jack Canfield work shop, but I was intrigued to find out the wealthiest, progressive people had vision boards! I believed I was "creating" my future, and this book helped me see money as another form of creative energy. It began my use of vison boards.

The week of my graduation, I was surprised to arrive at work to find a heartfelt congratulations card. It contained a huge tip. Duane was proud of my accomplishments and hard work. I valued his opinion; his endorsement meant a lot to me.

Earlier that week, I had received a surprise that really shook me. My client, Carol, was my absolute favorite client. She epitomized an angel spirit to me. Sweet, kind without guile, I just loved her. I loved cleaning and making her house beautiful for more reasons than pay. She had a way of making you feel special.

The first thing I saw when I walked in the door that day was a huge present sitting on the counter. It dominated the space; it was impressive! A bright red gift bag, it stood 3 feet tall with lovely tissue paper festooning the top. I thought, "Wow, that is something! Whoever deserves that, is someone special!"

As I worked, I glanced at the present, curious as to the contents of such a beautiful, big present, thinking what a surprise for someone. As I gathered my tools to leave, the phone rang. It was Carol. She asked if I had I found my graduation present? *What?!* That present was for *me?* I felt weak. I had to sit down to open it.

With tears, and in complete awe, I sat with the hugeness of what it signified. It was a physical representation, a validation of all the late nights and early mornings, sweat, stress, and hard work I had put into this goal. It was special, and significant, and an awesome present . . . it was a fire-engine red Pendleton blanket.

Any gift that came out of that bag would have been wonderful, but to a Native American, a Pendleton is almost a sacred object. The enormity was not lost on me. I treasure it to this day.

I had achieved another one of my goals. I had my fire science degree. I had paid for and taken the grueling International Code Council exam to obtain my certification. No small feat, this was a test in building and fire codes that was a timed, proctored process. It required knowing the international building codes and the fire codes and, more importantly, being able to navigate these two extensive books along with National Fire Protection Association code references thrown in.

It was not something that a volunteer would usually do, but I was determined to be a qualified candidate. I had worked so hard to be able to apply for our Deputy Fire Marshal position at District #3. It was my dream. It was my plan, when Deputy Roy Brown announced his retirement, that I would be ready to throw my hat in the ring for the vacated position. It was a crushing blow when the day came, and I found I could not apply.

The district announced it would be recruiting "in-house." Volunteers were not considered in-house and therefore; I did not qualify. The fact that the office workers could apply and get offered such a position, was frustrating. At a loss, I wondered, "Now what would I do?" I have come to learn that when one door closes, it is for a reason.

"You know, OSFM has an opening; you should put in an application." Deputy State Fire Marshal Charlie Chase and I were taking a break from the Fire Prevention booth at the Jackson County Fair. Every year our local fire cooperative partnered with the Oregon Department of Forestry to provide free fun and fire safety education, as part of the Rogue Valley Fire Prevention Cooperative, an interagency nonprofit fire service organization.

Composed of state and federal agencies engaged in fire prevention and public education, the Cooperative promotes the exchange of ideas, programs, and resources in the area of fire prevention and public education. For many years, this group occupied and provided a free prevention area located at a prime location near the ponds at the Jackson County Fairgrounds. As the Deputy State Fire Marshal for Southern Oregon, Charlie was there working a shift.

I had seen the posting for the Office of the State Fire Marshal in the *Gated Wye*, a monthly newsletter for the Oregon Fire Service. I had been looking at want ads now that I had my degree, and it was clear our district would not let volunteers apply for my longed-for position of Deputy Fire Marshal.

When I got the application, I saw that it had a box to check that indicated the applicant "will work anywhere in Oregon." That was a problem. I couldn't do that. I loved where I lived in Southern Oregon, and I didn't want to move 'anywhere.'

Charlie explained that the position that was being vacated was located in Klamath Falls, just over the hill from Medford. There would potentially be the opportunity for transfer in the future. The deputy for the area was retiring, and best yet, it would be an entry level position. Entry level, what was that?

The requirements for a deputy state fire marshal were very stringent and specific. The catch-22 is that anyone meeting the full requirements would have to already be a fire marshal. The pay difference between a state fire marshal and a local deputy was significantly lower. In the recent past, they had been struggling to fill vacant positions.

Recognizing that there were applicants that had all the desirable attributes but not the time on the job, the Fire Marshal's Office created an "entry level" position. The thought was to 'grow' this person into full deputy status within 2 years. The Office had done just that one time previously; I could be the second.

I had spent my time observing how our department and our neighboring departments functioned as a hierarchy, with a fire marshal who is the manager of the Fire and Life Safety Division and deputies who work under that fire marshal. I wasn't sure just how the deputy state fire marshal fit in to the picture. What is the state fire marshal's relationship to the districts if they have a local fire marshal? How did they fit together?

I contacted the state Fire Marshal's office, applying for a "job shadow" appointment so I could find out. I became Charlie's shadow.

As a shadow it was my mission to find out everything I could about, not only the job of the deputy, but the big picture of how the head of the fire service worked in the state of Oregon.

Chapter 12

Protecting citizens, their property, and the environment from fires and hazardous materials.

– Oregon State Fire Marshal Mission 2001

The Oregon Office of State Fire Marshal was established in 1917 with the State Insurance Commissioner serving as ex officio State Fire Marshal. In 1963, the Legislative Assembly separated the Office of State Fire Marshal from the insurance commissioner and placed it directly under the governor. Another legislative change in 1971 incorporated the OSFM under the Department of Commerce and provided for the appointment of a state fire marshal and the establishment of a separate administrative office.

The Department of Commerce dismantled in 1987, and the OSFM transferred to the Executive Department. It remained there until 1993, when it was transferred to the

State Police in an effort to consolidate public safety responsibilities in Oregon.

The first officially appointed state fire marshal was C. Walter Stickney in 1963. With ten divisions, including Fire & Life Safety, the State Fire Marshal's office oversees our state operations.

Administration Services directs agency budgeting, legislative relations, adoption, and interpretation of the state fire code, fire service mobilization planning, work force development, and strategic planning. In addition to standard office functions including reception and facilities services, staff provide administrative support to the Governor's Fire Service Policy Council and the Oregon Fire Code Committee. (www.oregon.gov/osp/programs/sfm/pages/default.aspx)

All fire marshals in the state, or the fire chief if there is no fire marshal, are considered by law as assistants to the state fire marshal. There are varying configurations of fire departments across the state:

1) The all-volunteer department; folks who willingly give their time and effort to support the community without compensation.

2) The combination department, which has some budget to work with and supplements personnel with volunteer support, and may have a fire marshal.

3) The fully funded departments that may or may not have a volunteer program and usually have a fire marshal.

The latter departments had the resources and manpower to establish a division of fire and life safety. These departments could apply to the state for what is called 'exempt status.'

For a department in the State of Oregon to attain exempt status, it must show and produce documentation that they meet stringent requirements, and that they conform to the state and national standards, specifically addressing the Fire and Life Safety unit.

The exemption represents a status of quality and also allows departments to locally modify code requirements. There are only nine departments currently in Oregon that have been allowed this status. In Southern Oregon, I was familiar with two: FD3 and Medford Fire and Rescue. (Ashland Fire & Rescue also met these requirements, but had not applied).

I thought back to my days at Gold Hill Fire when we had relied on the state for safety materials, free training, and direction. The state was the overseer of all fire departments in the state of Oregon. It began to make sense.

What exactly, as a deputy state fire marshal, would I do day-to-day? If I were to apply, what would that look like? What is the difference between a local deputy fire marshal and a state fire marshal?

From the state website, I learned they did–well, everything! The performance requirements listed not only all the duties that I had learned that our two deputy fire marshals at FD3 did: inspecting, investigation, plan reviews, education of public and fire personnel, prevention, but also what our fire marshal did as the chief of the Fire and Life Division.

I read the job requirements: "Manage a large geographical area with multiple small districts, provide education to not only the public, but to fire personnel, assist fire departments, enforce the fire code, meet with planning departments to review plans, inspect structures that the public occupies, including prisons and hospitals."

There was more: "Conduct fire investigations, testify in court, attend fire chief meetings, support the local fire cooperative, give interviews to the media, and respond to wildfires during fire season, which could include filling roles during large fire events, conflagration.

The role of the deputy fire marshal was in *managing* those large fire incidences, not fighting fire as I did in past large fire events. It was intimidating . . . but a challenge as well. I figured I would check it out.

The position that would be opening was located in Klamath Falls.

I had only been to Klamath Falls once since I had moved to southern Oregon. There hadn't been much to remember of the visit. It was a Sunday, and the town seemed sleepy, full of mosquitoes, and closed down.

I would later find out the swarms that looked like smoke billowing off the lake were called midges. Technically not a mosquito, midges are teeny-tiny bugs that clog areas of the Klamath Basin, especially along Upper Klamath Lake, and irrigation canals each summer. These midge larvae feed on the shallow, nutrient-rich waters of the Klamath aquatic ecosystem. Thankfully, they don't bite.

I decided to go back for a second look. I had secured permission to ride along with the retiring deputy to discover exactly what I would be in for if I applied. Driving over Hwy 140, I wondered, will I be able to commute through the winter?

On a good day the scenery is gorgeous, with alpine type meadows ringed by aspen trees, and the quiet lake spread out as you round the hill, winding around the edge of the lake. I wondered how serene and beautiful it would be in blizzard weather.

My initial response to the area was, "Oh my, can I live here!?" It seemed so dry and plain. Driving hours and hours with retiring Deputy Floyd Wilton, I was awed at the distances he traveled to assist with fires, inspecting schools for the smallest of towns in places called "Christmas Valley" and "Plush."

In time, I would come to find the beauty of, not only the area, but the people as well. I listened as Floyd described responding in the winter to places remote, meeting with chiefs late at night, and so on, and he assured me I would be glad to have the four-wheel drive truck that was provided.

Deputy Wilton had been the Klamath and Lake County deputy so many years that people found it difficult to remember who came before him. I found him to be a hilarious storyteller and great guide as we set out on a journey to see *some* of the district; we would not be able to cover even half of it all in one day.

Klamath County had a total area of 6,136 square miles (of which 5,941 square miles is land and 194 square miles is water. It is the fourth largest county in Oregon and has just under 70,000 population. Lake County covers 8,275 square miles and has an estimated population of 8,130 residents. The economy consists primarily on agriculture, timber, livestock, and government.

As we drove, Deputy Wilton painted a picture describing each of the local departments, and what they expected and required from the state. The vastness of the area was intimidating, how did he get it all done? Explaining, he stated this was the best part of the job: you get to figure that out!

Besides the licensed facilities which had a specific time frame for inspection, it would be up to me to set my own schedule for inspections. Fire investigations, of course, took priority and would come unannounced.

Later, driving home, I pondered the feasibility of working in Klamath, and literally covering Klamath and Lake counties.

Could I live there? How would I live there? I agonized; I had my doubts. I discussed it with my family.

Ben calmed me down, and we tried to imagine how it would work. We decided we could keep our home in the Valley; he would work and live there until I could transfer back. I decided if it was meant to be, I would be able to transfer in one year. We could do it. Ben was working steady. I could find housing and commute home on the weekends. I closed my eyes, I took a deep breath, I checked the "will work anywhere" box, and submitted my application.

What came next was an exercise in patience. The first step in the process came in the form of a notification letter that arrived stating "Congratulations; you've made it to the next step." Next, came a nerve-wracking phone interview with the state fire marshal, the manager of the Fire and Life Safety unit, the Code Division deputy, and at least one person from human resources.

Explaining my fire background experience, all the investigation time spent, and that I had already, as a volunteer, secured my fire code certification, I hoped for the best. The fact that I had kept records of every fire investigation I had worked on, that I was an active member of the Arson Investigation Association and member of the Fire Marshal Association, helped. It showed that I was ready to take on the task of working my way to deputy status.

I was elated and overjoyed when the invitation arrived for me to come to Salem to participate in an all-day assessment process held at the Office of the State Fire Marshal. The nervousness grew as the day approached. Ben was nervous too, worried that his past might reflect badly on me. He was supportive and told me he knew I would do well.

All I could be told was that the assessment process would consist of several stations that would (1) test my abilities to manage my time, (2) address code issues, (3) deal with customers and chiefs, (4) present information to a group, (5) conduct a panel interview, and (6) present a fire investigation case explaining in detail how I determined the origin and cause of the fire. "Piece of cake/can of corn" as my fellow EMT student and friend, Samantha, would say . . . not!

On the day of the skills assessment, we changed stations and worked on a code test in between calls. I didn't know what to expect going in and didn't have a real clue of how I did. It was all such a blur of activity. In the future, when I became a deputy, helping conduct this hiring assessment would be fun. I would look forward to being on the testing side of that process. It was a great way to get an overall impression of candidates' abilities and, most importantly, their attitude.

At this point, having made it thus far, I was overjoyed and amazed I was still in the process. Later, I would learn I was doing well in the overall review of candidates, based in large part on my attitude and the fact I had worked so hard as a volunteer to gain not only experience, but fire code certification that was not easily obtained.

After many long days, I received "the call." They would like to advance me on to the background check. If I, the candidate, passed this rigorous investigation of all aspects of both my personal and professional life and background, I could be offered the position. To say the background check was extensive would be an understatement.

It was another long process within the process. Retired state police employees are hired to conduct these background checks.

Like a trained bloodhound, he tracked down and interviewed my fire chief, training officer, staff and personnel at the fire department, my fellow firefighters, my friends, family, and even the people in my neighborhood.

The Office of the State Fire Marshal is a division of the State Police. His job is to assure that any individual who might be considered for employment can meet the high level of respect and integrity that the Oregon State Police requires of all its employees. If I were to be hired as a deputy, I would be located within the State Police office in Klamath Falls.

Days went by, then weeks, then a month. I wondered when would this waiting end, one way or the other? I was sitting at the college coffee shop when I my phone rang; it was Acting State Fire Marshal Nancy Orr. "Congratulations, Michelle, we would like to offer you the position of Fire and Life Safety Specialist!" She continued on saying that she just knew I would do well and be a full deputy in no time. They would allot 2 years for a specialist to become a full deputy. I was floating on a cloud, terrified and elated, as I raced home to share my good news with my family.

Chapter 13

"These are days . . . you'll remember, never before and never since, I promise, will the whole world be warm as this. And as you feel it, you'll know it's true that you are blessed and lucky. It's true that you are touched by something that will grow and bloom in you.

–Natalie Merchant & the 10,000 Maniacs

My good news was spread even wider at an event that our district held every year, the annual district awards banquet attended by all the district personnel, special guests, the local state fire marshal, and volunteers. Accomplishments are acknowledged and awards presented. As volunteers, it is the time we might be recognized with a "volunteer of the year award" or gain some special mention alongside our paid compadres.

Following along with the agenda, the most esteemed Wes Claflin Award was given, and we had reached the "thank you for coming" portion of the night when our Fire Marshal Lou Guggliotta stood and began to speak. I came to full attention when I heard him say, "This person expressed a desire to change their life, this person has worked diligently . . . " Lesa and I looked at each other across the table wide-eyed, oh my gosh, he's talking about me!

"I am proud to say this person will soon be leaving the district to go to work for the Office of the State Fire Marshal . . . Michelle, will you please come forward?"

Surprised into action, I made my way to the front of the room. I was honored and completely overcome. I found myself being thanked for my service and praised for my accomplishment. I was presented with a chromed, beautifully mounted on wood, cut to 3 feet, short pike pole. The award read, "Fire and Life Safety Appreciation January 2001." A pike pole is a long, wooden-handled, spiked tool with a metal hook. It is used by firefighters for a variety of uses such as tearing down damaged ceilings.

I was honored to tears, walking back to my seat I heard, "Speech, speech!" As I walked back to the podium, I mentally thanked that person; I definitely had some thank you's that I wanted to share!

I don't remember the speech. Charlie, who had attended as the State Fire Marshal Deputy for Jackson and Josephine counties, told me later I did a good job. I hope I didn't miss thanking anyone that deserved my thanks. I do remember thanking first my family, then the district for providing the opportunities and support. I thanked our fire marshal, and especially our deputies, Brown and Shaw, for all the wisdom and knowledge that they so willingly had shared with me. I walked out floating on a cloud of happiness. This was really happening!

Frustration followed shortly after as I began my search for housing in Klamath Falls. It was truly destiny stepping in when our evidence technician stationed at Klamath Falls mentioned a friend was looking for a house sitter. It wouldn't be a solid solution, just the summer while she was gone, but I was desperate. Up until then, it had been a fruitless, discouraging search.

I was introduced to Elizabeth Buelna who would become not only a housing solution short term, but a great friend and housemate. The day my daughter, Teresa, and I drove to her log house in Keno, I was so relieved to see trees and water. She lived by the river! My spirit sang, I could definitely live here.

Elizabeth was a wildlife biologist that spent the summer flying and counting birds in Canada. Open, friendly, and welcoming, I felt an instant connection with her. I was impressed to learn that she, her brother, and father had basically finished the beautiful log home she lived in. She was thrifty, smart, and fun.

I would house sit for the summer months while she was gone flying. She had everything automated for feeding and watering, but didn't want her dogs to be lonely. Lucky me I got to pet the dogs and live in a gorgeous log home. Not only did I stay for the summer, but the arrangement worked so well I would stay until I moved back home, one year later.

I began my career with the State of Oregon on February 2, 2001. Retired deputies Floyd Wilton and Al Higgins were assigned to get me acclimated. They would introduce me to my two county districts. I would laughingly refer to these two mentors as my 'tormentors.' They showed me the ropes, challenged me, and pushed me to do my best.

Twice a year, all deputies would attend an in-service week at the main office in Salem. Fall and spring the in-services were held like clockwork. It was at the in-service that I was formally introduced to all my fellow deputies. Deputies throughout the state converged for the week. This time was spent planning and conducting annual gear checks and tests, and generally to attend to the business of the office. I looked around, trying to absorb all this new information.

The deputies were located strategically, spread out all over the state. Most of the offices were located within Oregon State Police patrol offices. They were a diverse group, each reflecting the areas they covered from Richard, the deputy from Ontario in cowboy boots, to Charlie, and to "Downtown Keith Brown" from Coos Bay who always dressed in suits.

There were 12 men and myself. This dynamic would change when Kristina Deshaine was hired in July. I had heard all about Krissy from Charlie. Charlie was a visionary for the future in the fire service and was a champion for women who were qualified to do the job. He prophesized back then that our Chief Deputy Nancy Orr would someday be State Fire Marshal.

He had urged both Krissy and me on to pursue our careers. Krissy was a short blond with a sassy cut to match her quick wit. I loved her down to earth, don't-beat-around-the-bush attitude. Her cute look could fool you; she didn't take any guff.

Kristina, like me, grew up with brothers and male cousins. She could hang with the guys and sometimes cuss like a sailor. She had a fire background and had served in the air force. We became friends immediately.

Only two deputies in the state besides John Caul, the codes deputy located in Salem, shared an office: Charlie for Jackson and Josephine counties and Deputy Mark Moran. Mark was the first "entry level" to be hired. He was a specialty deputy and now, a health care deputy.

It was good to see a familiar face. We had worked fires together in Jackson County. Steady as a rock, quiet, and very knowledgeable, with warm, brown eyes that turned dead serious when dealing with a situation that called for it.

Health care deputies were considered "specialty deputies." They were certified in National Fire Protection Association 101 Life Safety Code and had specific duties governed by federal regulations. It was a jumble of information. I would learn much, much more about this program in the future.

As the second person hired as an entry level, I quickly learned as I listened to the conversations around me, that this was a bone of contention for the senior union deputies. I felt myself bristling, listening to "dumbing down the process and lowering the bar" comments, all accompanied by quick additions of "no offense meant." I realized some believed I had been hired either because I was a woman, because I was a minority, or both, and because they had 'dumbed' down the process.

Remembering all I had gone through to be here; I felt my face flush. Thinking of how I had worked my tail off to be here with a firefighter background, I had worked harder to prove myself and my capabilities *because* I was a woman! I was determined to be the best deputy I could be. Later as a part of that union, I would understand the thought process, and understand the comments truly were not personal.

The office requires the best of the best. Even the minimum job requirements for a full deputy are stringent, not only with hands-on time on the job, but code certifications and up-to-date training that is ongoing.

The applicant would need five years of full-time fire service experience. This must include two years of full-time code enforcement and one year of fire-cause investigation.

An associate's degree in fire prevention, fire science, or related fire service field may substitute for up to two years of the required experience, but will not substitute for the code enforcement and fire-cause investigation experience.

A bachelor's degree in fire service administration or fire protection, fire science, or closely related fire service field may substitute for up to two years of the required experience, but again will not substitute for the code enforcement and fire-cause investigation experience.

You must possess a valid International Code Council Fire Inspector II certification and a valid ICC Fire Plans Examiner certification, or obtain one within six months of appointment. Credit for part-time or volunteer fire service experience was prorated based on a 40-hour workweek.

(http://www.sfm.state.or.us/)

Unfortunately, the best of the best, the folks who are fully qualified, are typically already employed doing the job. Most folks that would apply were those looking to relocate. And to make it more difficult for recruitment, the pay scale difference between a state employee and a locally hired deputy were significant.

The entry level 'fire prevention specialist' would allow the office to grow a person into the requirements for the deputy level. Given my time working with my district, my passion for fire investigation, and the fact I had obtained my code certification as a volunteer, I was much closer to gaining my goal of attaining full deputy status.

I left Salem with a ton of books and a head full of information. Every day was an adventure. The feeling of, "I have the best job ever!" never left me in the 15 plus years I worked for the State.

The flow of setting my schedule, choosing when and where I wanted to inspect, agreed with me. The fact that things could change at a moment's notice and I would be on my way to a fire investigation, fueled my excitement for adventure. My first months on the job were a whirlwind of learning new programs, meeting fire chiefs, and absorbing all the information Floyd could download from years of history and relationships.

A fire deputy state marshal is a liaison to a multitude of other aspects of the position. A deputy must have a good working relationship with not only the fire chiefs and marshal, but the building officials, government officials, local police, juvenile workers, seniors with disabilities, foster care, the list goes on and on. At times the responsibility felt intense: how does one person get all this work done? The answer of course is, you don't. I was surprised to learn many small "mom & pop" business type occupancies had not been inspected in *years*!

Ah, now some of the conversations at the deputy in-service planning session made sense. We, the State, had to prioritize the work load; there was no way every occupancy could be inspected yearly.

Add to that, our own statistics-gathered fire trends would dictate where energy would be spent. Each year these planning sessions would uncover the latest trends. One year, mill fires would be added to our plates. Later it was night clubs that became a priority, as a direct result of the Station night club fire in Rhode Island.

With 18 deputies to cover the vast areas that did not have large fire departments, there was a lot of work to be done. In all the years I worked for the Fire Marshal's office, I could only count two short periods that all those positions were filled. This meant there was always an overflow of work for the deputies closest to the vacant areas.

My days were full: learning new programs, conducting inspections, and responding to fire investigations with Al and Floyd. Coming into the job with my code certification under my belt and the experience I received at FD3, I completed my task books and earned my badge in 8 months' time. It was a proud day when then Fire Marshal Robert

Garrison pinned my gold badge on my chest at a small ceremony at the Salem office.

Every day was a new experience and challenge. I was doing what I loved and loving life. Each day unfolded, never the same and always something happening. It was an unbelievable day when the world stood still on September 11, 2001.

"Oh my god, check this out!" I was headed out the door for work when Elisabeth's voice stopped me. We watched as the television played out the horrific sight of the plane crashing into one of the Towers. What the heck is going on?! Driving to my office, I listened as the news grew worse. When I got to the State Police office, we watched on a small television set pulled into the briefing room. The day passed in a surreal haze, it felt wrong to *not* be doing *something,* it felt wrong to be doing regular, *everyday* duties. I have heard people describe this feeling after they have lost a loved one, how can the world keep spinning and life go on when such a momentous change has occurred?

Our world would never feel quite the same in the aftermath. It would change our office, as well. We were almost instantly thrown into a pay freeze and mandatory days off without pay in our effort to reduce the budget. Although I achieved deputy status in October, which came with a step increase, my pay would never be right. I was so happy to have such a great job, I didn't care.

Later with some time and wisdom, I would see how the folks hired in this manner, brought in at entry level, were affected in pay and status, and why the union folks balked. The practice of hiring this way was discontinued soon after.

Chapter 14

If you talk about it, it's a dream, if you envision it, it's possible, but if you schedule it, it's real.

–Tony Robbins

When I made deputy status, my two mentors, Floyd and Al, fully retired. I was on my own. It would be a year of first experiences. Right away I had my first experience of real snow driving.

In the Rogue Valley, we *might* get a couple days of snow on the valley floor. *Maybe* a few inches on the ground that would make the world look beautiful and quickly melt. Klamath Falls in 2001 was what old timers called the "way it used to be" with three feet of snow, easy. I learned about dry snow and wet snow and using markers to stay on the road in whiteout conditions. It was an adventure all right!

It was now up to me to figure out my district. Each day would bring a multitude of calls, requests for code information, help with training, requests to attend meetings with local fire officials. I was loving it!

Busy, busy all the time. So much to learn! One day a request came to check out a complaint at a foster care home in the area. Knowing the statistics that most fire deaths occur in homes, I set out to meet with the caregiver.

This was a residence licensed to house disabled adults, and the provider had a question about wood paneling that had been installed. Speaking with him, I learned just how many of these care homes existed in Klamath and Lake Counties. I was taken aback; holy cow, inspecting them would be a full-time job by itself!

I was relieved and somewhat concerned to find that, by statute, neither we nor the locals had authority or responsibility to inspect all of these particular residents. I learned Department of Health and Human Services (DHS) has authority over these occupancies. They have their own people who inspect the homes with a check list for fire and life safety.

I was surprised that unless a DHS employee contacted us with a direct request to assist them, they were not in our authority. They must do a pretty good job because I think we have been lucky not to have any large incidences of fire deaths in private, licensed, foster care homes. Many are now retrofitted with fire sprinkler systems for fire and life safety.

Our office kept the statistics for fire fatalities. I now understood on a deeper level that over the years of reporting fire deaths, the number one place people die in a fire incident is in their home.

I had learned about fire sprinklers as a firefighter studying fixed systems. Now, reviewing plans involving fire sprinklers in public occupancies, why weren't they required in the places people were dying every year? This would become a central issue over the years, this problem of no sprinkler systems, especially in residential occupancies.

In the state of Oregon, your home is your castle. Your freedoms are protected under the Fourth Amendment, governed by state law. I lived by our bible, the fire code. As a Fire Marshal, my authority for inspection covered the places that the public frequent and occupy.

Navigating the fire and building codes is a feat all its own. The intricacies of interpreting code are many. Add to that the fact that the international code is on a 3-year cycle of change, the state on a 2-year cycle of review, and amendment process. We, as state fire marshals, are usually looking to assist with the hard-to-find answers.

The international fire code is brought to the State Fire Marshal's office to be reviewed. The State led that process with the input and hard work of officials from across the state, meeting at the Salem office for months of review and revision before the latest edition is adopted.

I would call our code guru, John Caul, "Is this right, John?"

Canadian born, he would say in lively accent, "Check this section, look harder, *then* call me back!"

He made us better code 'dogs.' John would head the state codes division for most of my years with the state. We would miss him and his great way of expressing himself when he retired.

In a nut shell, the building code and Building Codes Division address the *how* of an occupancy. It addresses the details of how it is to be built. The fire code is a maintenance code. This code details how the building will be *maintained* once it is built.

The fire code, among many other things, addresses the nine main occupancy types that we inspect: assembly, business, mercantile, educational, hazardous, institutional, factory, storage, and miscellaneous. It is apt that the code book is red since many of the requirements are a direct result of an actual event in which lives were lost. The state laws require certain inspections, for example, for schools. The Fire Marshal's office determines priority of all others.

In the Coconut Grove fire of 1942, 200 individuals lost their lives trying to flee a nightclub after combustible decorations spread fire quickly throughout. The fire created codes relating to types of combustible decorations, emergency lighting, and exit issues.

The Great Adventure Haunted House Fire in New Jersey in 1984 resulted in changes and additions for special amusement occupancies. The fire was ignited by someone using a lighter to see better. The lighter set foam and other wall coverings on fire.

My main daily duties were conducting inspections and assisting our customers with code enforcement; however, fires always took priority. Per Oregon law ORS21, "all fires in the state of Oregon will be investigated." I was excited when I was contacted by 911 dispatch for a suspicious fire.

Initially, investigations of origin and cause determination can be made by the fire department personnel. The fire investigators' job is to determine the origin of the fire–the exact physical location within the area of origin where a heat source and the fuel came into contact, resulting in a fire or explosion. If the cause cannot be determined, they will request a State Deputy. If the fire is in any way suspicious, an arson detective will be summoned.

Together, the investigators work to determine the cause of the fire, was it an accident or arson? If the fire was determined to be arson, detectives would then pursue the party or parties responsible for adjudication. Arson is defined as "the willful or malicious burning of property (such as a building), especially with criminal or fraudulent intent."

Like the deputy state fire marshals, the Oregon state arson detectives are located around the state with large geographical areas to cover. Working closely with the district attorney, they will take the case through the justice system to its conclusion.

My report would be a part of what makes up a complete picture of the events of the crime. In this case, and many others I would prepare for court, show up with photos and diagrams in hand only to have the defendant, when faced with all the evidence gathered against them, plead guilty. It was a letdown, but surely a testament to the hours of work by many that go into these cases.

The fire was located in a log home in the small town of Bly. Located in southeastern Klamath County, slightly west of Lake County along Oregon Route 140, by highway it is about 37 miles west of Lakeview and 50 miles east of Klamath Falls.

Bly's claim to fame is that it is the site of the only fatalities of World War II in the contiguous United States due to enemy attack. (On May 5, 1945, a Japanese balloon bomb exploded as it was being pulled from the woods by curious picnickers.) https://cs.stanford.edu/people/eroberts/courses/ww2/projects/fighting-vehicles/other-axis.htm

After being contacted by our 911 dispatch with a request for investigation, I arranged to meet the local chief and our Southern Oregon arson investigator at the scene. The fire chief met us, relaying what information he had, and the "red flags" that made him think this might be arson.

In the initial interview, the occupant was asked standard questions, "When did he leave? Did he cook breakfast before he left? Was the dryer running?" Things that might be accidental causes. The physical evidence, coupled with eyewitness accounts, would be studied and usually fall together eventually like a puzzle.

In all my schooling and investigation classes, I had listened to my instructors talk about "that" fire. The fire where you process the scene and find . . . well, a bunch of nothing. If you think about it, right now most of us have lots of "stuff" in our houses like the stuff on the dresser, loose change, odds and ends. We have clothes hanging in our closets . . . stuff!

There are usually always remains. In total or in part there will be coins, metal objects, clothing that falls and is somewhat protected until at last the whole house is consumed. Even after a total burn, there will be remains of metal objects to be found. Reconstruction is a big part of the fire investigation. Cleaning, sweeping, out the debris that has fallen into the scene, examining the patterns and remains, they all tell a tale.

We went to work. Gathering data, we documented interviews from the occupant and firefighters. An important piece of the fire puzzle is the report of the first person to see the fire. Fire at a very basic level of behavior has a pattern. Wherever it originates, it will spread up and out, growing as the heat and flame consume combustibles and intensify.

There are many factors that influence the behavior: ventilation, building configuration, materials burning. It is very unusual, not impossible, but unusual to have multiple areas of origin.

Interviews with the reporting party, firefighters, and witnesses, one with a partial video, indicated multiple areas burning. We gathered our tools and began processing the fire scene. Examining the physical visible remains of the structure, we studied the areas least burned to most burned and the patterns created.

Sifting through the debris in the bedroom, I was surprised at the lack of normal household "stuff." There were some items, but didn't the occupant swear there were guns under the bed? Guns don't go away in a fire; the stock will burn, but metal will still be left. The reasons this might not be the case are considered, was this a burglary with a fire set to cover the crime?

Hypotheses are formed. Based on physical evidence, they will be ruled in or out. The time of the call is always significant. In this fire, the occupant had "just left," as a witness directly across the street would testify to. Another witness would report seeing the occupant loading items from the home just the day before.

Multiple areas of origin were confirmed, all the physical remains examined and documented with photos, along with taped observations that would become my fire report.

Riding with Arson Detective Ryan Fields, obtaining a search warrant, looking for evidence, and learning more about the law enforcement side of arson was exciting!

Luckily, our arsonist was not very competent, to put it nicely. He would give a damning deposition, which in the legal world is the point of no return; there would be no redacted statements. It is not against the law to burn your own items; the crime occurs when you attempt to collect fraudulent insurance money or put others at risk.

The arsonist continued to tell his story insisting on his innocence. At one point before his actual arrest, he would storm into my office, arrogant, belligerent, and complaining loudly. That behavior got him escorted out of the building by our very large, very intimidating "there will be no nonsense in his office" Sergeant.

He would later that day leave a vicious voice mail that ended with a "I'll kill you, you witch," (something like that, anyhow!) threat on my answering machine. He ultimately was convicted, all the while trying to pin the whole fire on his wife.

When I began my career with the Oregon Office of State Fire Marshal, we had two arson detectives located at the Oregon State Police Headquarters in Central Point.

One detective was the arson dog handler. He and certified arson canine, "Kent," responded across the state wherever they were needed. I would work with many of the detectives in the state and utilized Kent, the arson dog, on numerous fires.

As the newbie, this was one of my first opportunities to work closely with Arson Detective Ryan Fields. Detective Fields had been one of the instructors at the investigation class that ignited my passion to be an investigator. Now we were working together!

Over the years, I would attend training and work with Detective Fields, as well as many of the other detectives located around the state. Eventually, we would co-instruct the fire investigation classes at Rogue Community College. Education is ever on-going in the fire science field. Later, Detective Fields would retire from Oregon State Police to begin his own successful private fire investigation practice.

New information and the advancing state-of-the-art technology required us to be ever-evolving in our knowledge. As a deputy, I would be required to keep up-to-date; a student throughout my career.

The year 2001 found me making my first visit to the National Fire Academy. The National Fire Academy is the crème de la crème for training of fire and fire emergency response. I was urged to go because it would be good training and a unique experience.

The National Fire Academy is one of two schools in the United States operated by the Federal Emergency Management Agency (FEMA) at the National Emergency Training Center (NETC) in Emmitsburg, Maryland. The application had to be made carefully because acceptance is not guaranteed. It was a strict process in which reference letters had to be obtained and submitted in a specific time frame.

I was accepted to attend the Fire Investigation course. Doing my research, I was surprised to learn that attendees often got together on the weekend to go into Washington, D.C. Washington, D.C.?! Isn't that where the Smithsonian Institute is located? I was elated! What a bonus!

I had 'visioned' that someday I would fulfill my bucket list dream to visit this unimaginable museum. I never imagined *how* that would happen, just that it would. Now I would be seeing this dream come true. Not only would I be attending amazing training and getting to travel, but it would prove to be an incredible immersion in history as the Academy was only miles from the famed battle site at Gettysburg, as well.

I had never been to the East Coast. I am not sure what I expected. It was an amazing surprise to find the area so incredibly beautiful, lush, and green. The campus was a huge array of historical, barn-red brick buildings spread out over a 105-acre span.

Operated and governed by the United States Fire Administration (USFA) as part of the U.S. Department of Homeland Security, the campus also includes the Learning Resource Center (LRC) library, the National Fire Data Center, and the place where a grateful nation honors its fallen fire service heroes at the National Fallen Firefighters Memorial Park. The Academy was established with free training and programs that are taught at the campus in Emmitsburg and throughout the nation.

The National Fire Academy was born of then President Nixon's decision in 1971 to assemble a 20-member panel of experts in the field of fire protection to study the country's alarming fire problem and the related needs of the American fire services. This group became known as the National Commission on Fire Prevention and Control (NCFPC).

The NCFPC and its staff published a report titled, *America Burning,* on May 4, 1973. This report would be the first publication that seriously recommended "home fire sprinklers," a subject that would become Oregon's and my own personal mantra in the future.(www.usfa.fema.gov)

They had been working on this home fire sprinkler thing awhile! Perforated piping came into use the 1800's. Henry Parmalee was credited with inventing the first automatic heads to protect his pianos in 1874. Why were so many people dying in fires when we have this technology, I wondered?

Anyone who has ever attended the Academy will tell you the training is the highest quality. The campus had concrete-built "burn buildings." The buildings are utilized over and over after being reconstructed inside to simulate rooms of origin for students to investigate.

But it is the people you meet that make the trip unforgettable. In our class, the vocal accents I heard were a wonderful mix of eclectic verbiage and diverse working conditions. From the challenges of a fire marshal in Alaska who flies to her investigations and sometimes has to wait until the spring thaw to investigate, to the fire marshal in the Virgin Islands who works in the intense heat and humidity of the Caribbean, this was all fascinating to me. Our instructors were a mix of southern drawl and Boston accent, and hearing about "awks and spawks" had us smiling.

The first week passed quickly with evenings full of studying. When the weekend finally arrived, it was time for some fun and we headed to the Smithsonian. I was surprised you could spend a whole day in just one museum! We traveled as a group and saw as much as we could. It was amazing. The museums proved to be more than I could have imagined or could ever see all of in these days of pre-Google.

The Academy experience was incredible. Looking back as I sat at the graduation ceremony, I felt awed and immensely grateful to have had this opportunity. Once you have been accepted into the Fire Academy, it is easier to be accepted in the future. I would end up going back to the Academy three times in the coming years; and I always felt the same.

Chapter 15

Mount up! Regulators ready!
–"Young Guns" film

Almost one year to the day I was hired, my time spent as the Klamath and Lake County Deputy came to an end. From the day that I checked the box on my application that stated, "I would work anywhere," I had been visualizing and planning that I would be back in the Rogue Valley in one year. Yet when the opportunity came, I was surprised to find that the thought of giving up my district and leaving, was hard.

I had come to love the beauty of the area, the wildlife, and especially the people. The opportunity to move home showed up in the form of a memo. A position was opening for a health care deputy, to be located in our Central Point office. This person would share an office with Charlie, at the State Police headquarters.

"I don't know, health care deputies are different, what if I don't like it?" Charlie and I were discussing the position that was announced in the memo. I would definitely like living at home, but this federal program sounded so very restrictive.

The State Fire Marshal's office contracted with the feds to complete the Fire and Life Safety portion of the surveys they conducted. A specialty position, the deputies in the Health Care division spent their time overseeing this program, inspecting only health care facilities. Ensuring that these facilities complied with the rules for Medicare and Medicaid was their primary purpose. I was somewhat disappointed because I wouldn't have my own district to run. The decision was agonizing, professionally, but in the end, going home won out.

I packed up my office and left the beautiful log home in Keno. I made my rounds visiting all my fire departments, saying good-bye. I would miss the east side with its vastness, the incredible sprawling ranch lands, and wild life.

It was an interesting transition. Ben was used to doing things his way and having me home on the weekends. I was used to having freedom. It seemed like his house now. It changed the way we related. I was glad this separation didn't last longer.

Becoming a health care specialist, I was required to obtain additional certification. As a regular deputy state fire marshal, we were certified in the National Fire Code. This new position required learning the ins and outs of the Life Safety 101 Code. Filled with additional federal requirements, it *was its own animal to be tamed.* Facilities receiving federal Medicare and Medicaid dollars must meet the more restrictive requirements of this code, as well as the requirements of the building and fire codes.

I found myself traveling to Baltimore to get certified. The class itself was rigorous, and the trip itself a blast. It was surreal to walk at lunch break from class to see the harbor that, in 1812, defended itself from attack from the British. It was that scene that inspired Francis Scott Key to write the poem that would become the "Star Spangled Banner."

Back in class, I was surprised to find that I, with another deputy from Oregon were the only two actual fire marshals in a room of 100! In most other states, the feds contract with sanitarians to conduct the Fire and Life Safety inspections.

I was actually surprised and glad to find out the degree to which our seniors are being looked after. I was amazed at the process the federal surveyors went through for a typical survey.

In their process, a team of inspectors would enter a facility, which required a meeting with staff. They would commandeer a room and set up shop for a week or more depending on the size of the facility. The average was one week for a nursing home, but a hospital could last longer and require a larger team.

The health survey team would look at everything. Records were examined with a fine-toothed comb. Everything was inspected, from times to respond to a call button, to the tests for acceptable water temperatures.

Their primary job was to see that residents were being attended to regularly. It was comforting to know that if a complaint were issued, a survey would be forthcoming. These folks do an incredible job. I would join them and conduct my portion of the survey to add to a 3-inch binder of reports.

My primary job was the fire and life safety of the facility. My inspection would include checking obvious fire-related issues such as making sure they had serviced fire extinguishers easily accessible, and maintained records to show this. And more importantly, to inspect life safety systems such as smoke barriers and fire separations. Facilities like hospitals, nursing homes, and jails, places where occupants are impaired, or immobile and unable to respond in a fire situation, are the reason for the special requirements of the 101 Code.

Most of these facilities utilize a "defend in place" concept. The buildings are specially built, and carefully designed and engineered. Their plans have to be reviewed.

Because staff cannot evacuate everyone when there is a fire, the building, itself, is constructed to deal with a fire event. The plan must separate a large hospital into large safe areas, provide for movement within the building, and allow fire response to deal with a fire inside. This is all accomplished with rated fire walls, automatic smoke evacuation systems, and highly trained staff. The staff is key in moving patients to safe areas and knowing what to do in a fire emergency.

I had my own stack of paperwork, policy and procedure manuals, and staff training documents to review for my inspection. Many times, my visit would involve a surprise fire drill. The maintenance director was usually the person who tested staff with unannounced fire drills per the code. This would include a simulated fire in a room or area to create a visual test of response.

The staff many times view these drills as a nuisance, interrupting their very important work, because years may go by with no incident of fire. However, the maintenance directors are the key to keeping systems working and would appreciate a drill from the fire marshal to instill how important it is to practice.

In the beginning, there was still a lot of flexibility in the program, as far as planning of the inspections. Our coordinator sent the list of nursing homes and hospitals that I would be responsible for; it was up to me to set my schedule.

Nursing homes would be inspected yearly, within a window of time that would allow me to arrive unexpected and unannounced. They could not be expecting me. Federal inspections of hospitals were initiated by the feds every three years, or unless there was a complaint, per the state code.

I would make a plan. Setting out at the far north of my district, making my way down the coast on a two-day run, I inspected some very nice facilities, as well as some very old facilities needing many corrections. It was a great deal of driving, but I was seeing areas I had never seen. I enjoyed the freedom of travel.

Initially, in learning the process, I shadowed other health care deputies traveling all over the state. They were their own elite group within the office. Gayle Johnson was our official "cat herder," she had her hands full keeping everyone on task with the federal requirements. Her job was all encompassing, from keeping our information straight dealing with the various entities to keeping track of us. Her plate was always full. Our Safety Manager, headed up the program.

George and Richard were our senior deputies. Between the two of them, they could not only tell you all the history of our office, but quote code and past practices back to the beginning.

Driving the desolate highway to Ontario, I marveled at the vastness of the state, and how far it was for the deputy stationed here to come to Salem for our meetings. Once I became certified, I would cover the southern portion of Oregon.

Being a dedicated health care deputy meant just that. I still participated in investigation and training, still attended classes with other deputies, but I was dedicated to inspecting nursing homes, hospitals, assisted living, and other health care occupancies that were federally funded.

Now my life became one of enforcement. As a general deputy, I was used to and appreciated the friendly "educate our customer" method of inspections. Before, on regular occupancy inspections, we spent time with our customers explaining why the exit door needs to swing in the direction of travel, and why they would want to address fire safety concerns.

This was a new way of doing things. The program was strict with regulations, and time lines were tightly adhered to. There were fines involved if citations were not corrected. The time, I spent in health care was filled with federal mandates that seemed to change with every meeting. One month we approved locked exterior gates with the provision that staff all had a key in event of an emergency. The next meeting, we would get new marching orders that it wasn't allowed: gates had to have break-away devices.

I know that, much like events drive fire code requirements, these changes were probably due to a failure, but it was exhausting keeping up with what I considered excessive restrictions.

We have a low incidence of fires in nursing homes and hospitals, and I am sure this program is partly responsible for that. But it just wasn't my style. I longed for the days of educating folks and the freedom of running my own district.

I gained some of that freedom back after Charlie suggested that we propose a plan to our manager to help with state coverage. We were always a "man short" on the rosters of deputies. Only briefly did I see all our positions filled over the years. Change is constant, people leave, and filling positions was typically a long process. In looking at our map of coverage, we had our deputy stationed in Coos Bay covering Coos County, west Lane County, and Curry County all the way down to the California border.

We came up with a proposal that changed the response lines allowing Charlie to cover Josephine County and southern Curry County, with my district coverage consisting of Jackson County and healthcare.

Jackson County coverage, in reality, would consist of primarily the outlying small districts. Medford Fire District and Jackson County #3 were exempt jurisdictions and efficiently covered large areas of Jackson County with their staffed divisions.

Small towns like Prospect, Butte Falls, and Shady Cove, to name a few, at the time did not have a certified fire marshal or inspector to conduct inspections, investigations, and address new construction. There are many small communities that rely on the State Fire Marshal's office for those duties.

The districts have shifted many times since that change to try to accommodate our customers and fire departments over the years. But there were never enough deputies to go around regardless of the configuration.

Chapter 16

"It is not the critic who counts; not the man who points out how the strong man stumbles, or where the doer of deeds could have done them better. The credit belongs to the man who is actually in the arena, whose face is marred by dust and sweat and blood; who strives valiantly; who errs, who comes short again and again, because there is no effort without error and shortcoming . . .

–Theodore Roosevelt

Every year, all the deputies had required code update training to keep our certifications and knowledge current. One event, the Fire Marshal Round Table, was always co-hosted by our office and the Oregon Fire Marshal Association.

I was familiar with the Association. Lou, our fire marshal, was the president when I was a volunteer at FD3. I had joined in the year 2000 as a student, and I had become a full member upon my employment.

I had seen the Association's board in action at the annual training that the group held each year. Fire marshals and fire officials from all over the state and neighboring states, along with their forestry partners, came together to train, network, and discuss current fire issues.

Watching the effort, it took to provide this training, I was impressed at the dedication to improve and support all fire marshals and fire and life officials across the state.

Every year after the new Board is elected, the group holds a new member planning camp. The year I joined the group, they met in my area and I was able to attend.

I sat listening to the discussions: results of meetings, the latest trends affecting the fire service, the needs of our investigators. Observing the thought processes and forward thinking that went into planning a year of events . . . I was fascinated, this was cool. I thought I would like to be a part of this mission!

Founded in 1965, the Association's vision of saving lives and reducing loss through fire prevention efforts, and their mission to support the fire service and its stakeholders by providing education and forums for discussion, addressing current fire and life safety issues, has not changed.

I made it my goal to become a board member. It was 2005 when I achieved that goal. To become a board member requires running for a position, being voted in by the membership, and a commitment from your department to support you. It is a big commitment, a long-term commitment.

The first year I ran for a seat on the Board there were five others campaigning. The membership that year chose the fire marshal from McMinnville, Eric McMullen. Eric was a code-savvy go-getter, and we were lucky to have him.

The next year I ran again, gaining a director position on the Board. Typically, you enter the Board on a 3-year director level. From here, you have several years to work your way up to the president level, growing your experience along the way.

Typically, these years are meant to ready the member, to groom and grow them into the succeeding positions. This was not a 'typical' time in Oregon. The Public Employee Retirement System was going through some drastic changes. People who had not planned to retire for years suddenly decided to pull the plug before their retirement funds were affected.

As a result of this mass retirement, there were many changes, not only throughout departments in Oregon, but in our board makeup, as well. The normal progression was disrupted. A new precedent was set as board members moved up, not by years on the board, but by vacancies created by retirement.

Our incoming president was one of those retirees. Initially, he planned to serve his term, but in the end, he decided he could not dedicate the time needed and stepped down early. This caused concern because the process is such that members need to grow into their positions over time.

Eric, who was now second in command, stepped up. It may have been a quick ascent, but he took the mantle and became our new leader. This group did a great job making the transition for the association managing the changes. I was proud to be one of them, although uneasy, as the changes were causing quick ascents in the Board.

In an effort to address the problem, the Board (with member input) decided that instead of 1-year term, our president would serve a 2-year term. This would allow the group some time to meld and learn their positions. I was relieved. I had only been on the board 3 years and was already the vice president! I was just getting to know the extent of the work and time it really takes to represent our association, not to mention needing to get to know the many players that I would interact with as president. But this was not meant to be.

The annual business meeting and training for Oregon of 2008 was held at Salishan Conference center in Gleneden Beach. The days leading up to the annual banquet dinner had been busy, two meetings of elections and then the banquet swearing in of new officers. In between, time filled with more meetings and training.

Everything was going well until the knock at my door on the day of the banquet. I found our fearless leader looking contrite, "I can't take the presidency for a second year, I'm sorry, you're going to have to step up." Step up!?! It is the day of the banquet!

It was a shock. So much for the 2-year presidency idea. Despite feeling inept at what I didn't know, and feeling like I should know as the president, I would turn to those who went before and give myself permission to ask for direction.

Usually when a person gets the honor of becoming president, their family would attend, and there would be a nice speech prepared; it was a big deal. The speech! Holy cow! I had a couple of hours to come up with a speech and prepare to take over sailing the ship. That is how it is that I became president just 3 years into the process.

We had a very successful year due mostly to the efforts and hard work of the OFMA group. Mark Wilson, the fire marshal from Lebanon, and Eric, our outgoing president, were who I turned to for mentoring.

Each president had their stated mission for the year. My mission was to work on building relationships with our Building Codes Division officials and promote home fire sprinkler systems. I couldn't understand why there was a gap between us, and especially why many would oppose the fire sprinkler requirements. It was my extreme pleasure to represent my office and OFMA at the international code hearings held in Minneapolis that year. It was a big privilege to see the code process unfold in person, and to be a part of the process.

The United States relies on consensus code-development processes run by nonprofit associations to develop building and fire codes, among many others. The International Code Council develops model codes. The changes submitted are heard in session over several days and those in attendance cast their votes. I would attend, along with our manager, code division head, and two other deputies to vote on behalf of our office.

Sprinklers were the hot topic. There were two code changes regarding residential fire sprinklers: RB66, which would require new townhouses to be equipped with fire sprinklers upon adoption of the code, and RB64 which would require all new one- and two-family dwellings to have fire sprinklers.

Sprinklers were already required in Scottsdale, Arizona, and Prince George's County, Maryland, with 15 years of case studies showing why it made so much sense. The data showed how fast sprinklers responded while a fire was beginning to grow, with a minimal amount of water used. Less damage, no fire deaths!

Installing residential sprinkler systems in conjunction with smoke alarms reduce fire deaths by 97%, injuries to responders go down, it reduces insurance company payouts because of less fire damage (usually putting the fire out with one sprinkler activated), and saves water, using approximately one tenth of the water usage compared to a firefighting effort. (www.sfm.or.us)

I was surprised at the controversy that surrounded this topic. The controversy included accusations leveled by both parties for and against home fire sprinklers. The home builders were accused of providing travel assistance to members who might not otherwise be able to attend to vote against the sprinkler requirements, and the International Residential Code Fire Sprinkler Association was accused of doing the same for its members. New to the process, it seemed to me that it was not taken as a passion of the fire community wanting to save lives by utilizing home fire sprinklers, but more as a power play.

After many delays, the votes began. IRC Fire Sprinkler Coalition's residential sprinkler proposals were on the agenda as Items RB64-07/08 and RP3-07/08. RB64, which passed, made the residential sprinkler requirement for one- and two-family dwellings part of the 2009 edition of the IRC with an effective date of January 1, 2011. RP3 was approved with 73% in favor.

We were elated; we would have our home fire sprinklers! It would take time starting with new construction, but halleluiah, the future home owners would not be dying in their own homes!

I left with a sprinkler head paperweight for my desk, to remember the momentous occasion. I came to realize after we returned, the requirement was not a done deal. The building officials review and amend the international code just as we did with our fire code. Much to the fire service's dismay, the Building Codes Division in Oregon voted to amend the provision. Oregon moved that the sprinkler requirement would be by local adoption only. It was frustrating to those who knew what having sprinklers in homes can mean

Home fire sprinklers work and we know this from case studies. There has not been a single fire fatality in Prince George's County, Maryland (ordinance enacted 1986) in homes protected with sprinkler systems. There has not been a single fire fatality in Scottsdale, Arizona (ordinance enacted in 1992) in homes protected with sprinkler systems. (www.scottsdaleaz.gov/fire/residential-sprinkler)

There was a real disconnect between the Fire Service and the Building Codes Division on the matter in many areas of the state and country.

In Southern Oregon, we worked diligently to build relationships with our Building Code partners. We attended the monthly local Southern Oregon Code Council meetings and trainings. Charlie would even serve as the Southern Oregon chapter president before his retirement.

We and the local fire marshals in our area were lucky to have good working relations consulting with each other to save our customers time and, ultimately, money. We had a great building official in Jackson County. Ted Zuk displayed an even disposition and calm way of dealing with many of the issues we would work together on to resolve.

Josephine County building official, Robert Rice, served as president of our local chapter and sat on the Oregon International Code board. Always a pleasure to work with, Robert, like Ted and others in southern Oregon, saw the value of fire sprinkler systems.

It was not always the case with other deputies working in different parts of the state. I would find out so much more as the Oregon Fire Marshals Association president.

As a member of the Association, I had the honor and privilege to be approved to serve on the Department of Public Safety Standards and Training's fire (DPSST) policy committee. The fire policy seat that represented the Fire Marshal Association was an appointed position. As an applicant, I was required to have the approval of the governor. Representing our association, I attended state fire chief meetings, building official meetings; I was getting to see what was happening all over Oregon.

I was honored to serve two terms with the top representatives of the Oregon Volunteer Firefighters Association, Oregon State Firefighters Council, Oregon Fire District Directors Association, community college fire programs, Portland Fire

& Rescue, Oregon Fire Chiefs Association, Oregon State Fire Marshal, and the Oregon Fire Instructors Association.

DPSST implements minimum standards established by the Board on Public Safety Standards and Training for recruitment and training of city, county, and state police; corrections officers; parole and probation officers; fire service personnel; emergency telecommunicators; and private security providers. This body also certifies qualified instructors and inspects and accredits training programs throughout the state based on standards established by the Public Safety Standards and Training Board.

The mission of DPSST is to promote excellence in public safety through the development of professional standards and the delivery of quality training. Governed by a 24-member board and six discipline-specific policy committees, they serve more than 35,000 public safety constituents across the state.

My year as president passed quickly. Just about the time I was getting the hang of things, it was over. I went out with a bang. As the outgoing president, it was my job to set the stage for the end of the year annual banquet. I envisioned a gathering that included family.

All the people from our Salem office were invited. The conference attendees for the annual meeting training could attend and have an evening of old-fashioned fun. The event was special with my sister, Judy, bringing the grandkids, and my husband, Ben, stopping in as he traveled north with the big rig he now drove. He had been laid off of a job where he had worked and never missed a day for the past 8 years. After some time, he had gone to school graduating top in his class, then he obtained his commercial driver's license to go to work driving trucks. He seldom attended any of my events, so I was glad he made it.

Our local Albany deputy was contacted We organized a great barbeque. The Firefighters Association provided the giant grill, and OFMA board members did the cooking and serving. Music was provided by our local fire sprinkler company band. Gayle and the ladies from the office helped set up and decorate. The grand finale would be a fireworks display, cool way to end the evening.

At the time, 'ghost mines' were the latest, greatest concern on fire marshals' minds. I had gained permission from then Fire Marshal Randy Simpson to have a demonstration of this pyrotechnic as a learning tool for attendees and a, as we were holding our event at the Albany fairgrounds.

Invented by Chris Spurrell, a research chemist from Hawthorne, California, a 'ghost mine' is a pyrotechnic device which, as I understood it, would project a large, ethereal-looking, colored fireball into the sky. The effect is produced by mixing methyl alcohol with a pyrotechnic colorant. Since alcohol burns with a nearly invisible flame, all that is seen by the audience is a cloud of glowing color (the colorant) taking the shape of the invisible fireball.

To say the effect was impressive is to minimize how it actually looked when it was demonstrated. All the attendees at the annual conference had the chance to check out the setup and ask questions as we toured it earlier in the day. Some like me hadn't seen the effect in person. As the sun set and dusk approached, we all gathered to watch. The fire department was in attendance. Everyone was ready.

Located a distance away standing with my family, we watched as the firework display lit up the sky, bringing a great day to an end. Everyone oohed and ahhed. I could see people standing outside in their yards pointing and smiling having enjoyed the fireworks display. Then came the grand finale, the latest, greatest technology, the ghost bomb. It was so quick, yet it was far too long. It was impressive all right, a huge ball of fire. It was scary, atomic-like, and I wondered briefly if something went wrong.

No wonder the Fire Marshal in Roseburg wouldn't allow it to be used inside the fairground arena! People scattered, running for cover, car alarms sounded, children cried, and the 911 center started calling. In retrospect, I think we should have prepared the neighbors and audience better.

This ending heralded other endings.

Chapter 17

> *"Getting over a painful experience is much like crossing monkey bars. You have to let go at some point in order to move forward."*
>
> – C.S. Lewis

Life at home was changing. As a young girl, I had tried to mold myself to my husband. I wasn't that little girl anymore. Growing up felt like growing apart. I tried to join Ben in his love of motorcycles. I loved riding, but it was really *his* passion.

I always tried to support him being him. I was happy when he did the things he loved. I didn't realize how it led to a separateness. I cheered him on when he came home from the largest motorcycle swap meet in Las Vegas. He arrived home with parts and pieces, excited to make me a motorcycle from the ground up.

It was a great project for him, and it turned out beautiful. A '76 Sportster low-slung classic. He did a fantastic job. I was proud of his huge accomplishment. It was custom painted black with iridescent feathers on the tank that sparkled in the light. It was an amazing and fast piece of work.

My husband, Ben, had always had his old Shovelehead motorcycle. He was a true motorcycle man. That was the freedom he craved. I rode and loved the freedom of wind and speed, but more and more the freedom I longed for was the freedom to be me, to really know who and what that was.

Maybe it was a longing for change, I didn't know. I just knew I *wanted*. I loved our house, but I wanted more. I wanted a piece of property, a big garden, and I wanted to live near water. He was averse to change in any form. It was hard for him. His motto was, "If it ain't broke, don't fix it, and if it is broken, make do."

I felt I had more to do in life. I grappled with the guilt of it all. Was I just selfish? Did I really need more? Could I hurt our family, and what would happen to him if I chose to leave? The biggest, hardest thing to face: what would become of him without me? Was I in charge of that?

He loved our place in Gold Hill. He tried to love what I loved, and I tried to love what he loved. In reality those were two different things. We limped along, each pursuing our own passions and coming together on the most important events with our kids and grandkids.

Change was in the air. I was feeling it at home and at work.

The demands of the job requirements of our office and positions grew more and more every year. The investigation world was ever shifting. To keep up with the latest technology required constant, consistent training, and constant testing of old ways of doing things.

The scientific world was disproving and improving the evidence we had relied on in the past. " . . . It used to be . . . " was a common statement of that past as we attended presentations and studied new evidence regarding the phenomena of flashover. Old beliefs and ideas that were accepted in the past were now questioned and, in some cases, discarded as new evidence emerged.

Always schooling myself, I read, attended the latest classes, and adapted. Inspection required constant ongoing training. The codes changed every 3 years, and they needed to be reviewed and applied as consistently as possible throughout the state.

Then the Rhode Island Station fire changed the face of fire inspection for us. It raised the bar to a new level, setting into motion a change of how we did business in Oregon.

February 20th, 2003, the Station nightclub became the fourth deadliest nightclub fire in U.S. history. Over 400 people had gathered in the club to hear the music act, Great White, perform when a pyrotechnic set off by the band's manager ignited the walls of the stage, triggering a blaze that took just 6 minutes to engulf the entire facility (NFPA, 2006). The loss of 100 lives was attributed mainly to the pyrotechnics igniting the flammable sound-insulating foam. The high loss of life resulting from the fire spurred a number of changes to life safety codes across the nation.

The elements that contributed to the severity of this disaster were identified in an official report following the fire (NIST, 2005), which noted additionally that, had the Station been governed by fire and building codes, and had the codes been enforced, the contributing factors would have been addressed.

Lawsuits rained down like bullets in the aftermath of the fire. The Rhode Island fire marshal and the local fire inspector were named in these law suits. The inspector in past inspections had noted other violations; however, he neglected to note the polyurethane foam on the interior walls.

This begged the question, if now State Fire Marshal Nancy Orr was responsible for fire authorities in the State of Oregon, who were identified in statute "as assistants to the Fire Marshal," what, if any, bar was set to assure consistency of code enforcement?

Immediately, a task force was formed that included the office of the Oregon State Fire Marshal, the Oregon Fire Marshal Association, and selected code officials, who were tasked with the responsibility to review how, and to what level, inspectors in Oregon needed to be trained to conduct inspections. The task force would make recommendations to assure those folks conducting fire inspections were trained to an acceptable level. This would attempt to keep things consistent across the state.

The result was a new competency certification process statewide with the new requirements to be able to conduct inspections and give input for Fire and Life Safety, which became more work for the deputies as long-time fire chiefs. Many of them were volunteers with limited time for certification training, and they opted out. The state deputies would have to pick up the slack.

Officials were required to obtain Fire Plan Examiner certification to be able to give the building officials input. The fire service took it in stride as the deputies were some of the first to obtain the new certification. Charlie and I were at the top of our list.

There were also changes happening in our department. The office was again looking at drawing new lines for districts in an effort to provide better, faster coverage. Being a health care deputy meant that person traveled a large area inspecting, but was not assigned a specific district for management.

The proposal that Charlie and I had come up with to the Fire and Life Safety manager had been accepted. I would be a full deputy with a district again.

Jackson County had two large exempt departments. I would be covering the small department inspections and investigations and could still cover the health care inspections for the southern part of the state. I would over the years, cover Jackson, Klamath, Lake, Douglas, Coos, and Curry Counties.

Our plates were full as our neighboring deputy took a hiatus that turned into a forever hiatus after one year being gone, and we had to cover for him. I would eventually, and happily, make my way out of health care to cover this district.

When "Brother Keith Brown," the Coos Bay deputy retired, we found ourselves tag-teaming coverage of his area as our office worked to fill the position. This district was a challenging spot to fill. The office would go through the extensive process to hire, only to find out in short order the fit was not right.

We would have one, then another come and go, the last being from Las Vegas FD, who transferred to find her fit in McMinnville, until we finally recruited a local who really 'fit' the area. The fit is important because the people need a solid contact to call, someone who is part of the community and can respond quickly, and be a go-to for questions. I was happy to get back to doing what I signed on to do, be a deputy state fire marshal, and my experience continued to grow with some new realities.

Chapter 18

We didn't start the fire
No, we didn't light it
But we tried to fight it
– Billy Joel

It was a cold morning when I awoke to the call from our local district. They were on scene at a fire where two small children had perished. The medical examiner's office had removed the two victims, and they would like help with the investigation.

One of the first things we noticed was what a good job the fire department did, they were met with a steep drive and frozen weather, but we still had structure to work with. I was glad they had already removed the bodies of the children. Fire deaths of children were heartbreaking enough without seeing the small bodies.

It was a small, three-room, wooden cabin located approximately 30 feet from the main residence. We would soon hear the story by conducting interviews of how the mother put her infant and small toddler to sleep in the cabin. Then taking a child monitor to listen in on them, she went to the main residence to work on a computer.

I have a horrible image of fire, small at first, luminous, and oh so quiet, lazily snaking up the wall, very silent and sneaky. I see the smoke curling upward, wafting first across the ceiling of the rooms as the children slept, settling lower and closer, reaching out to fill two small airways. The blessing is they were asphyxiated before the fire would touch them.

Once a body is discovered in a fire, the medical examiner tests the victim's blood and tissues for carbon monoxide. Normal CO levels are less than five percent, but can be slightly higher in smokers. The CO level in asphyxiated victims ranges from 45 to 90 percent.

As a fire progresses, the CO level increases to 20 percent, and dizziness and confusion occur. At 35 percent, a loss of coordination and weakness ensues and disorientation increases. At levels of 50 percent or more, the victim experiences a loss of consciousness and, eventually, death.

There are sometimes obvious, visible signs that the person died from smoke inhalation: cherry red lips, soot in the airway. Depending on the condition of the body, there will be no sure way to know until the official cause of death is determined by the chief medical examiner.

It was always hard to deal with fatal fires because emotions are high, not only of the family of the deceased person, but for firefighters and other responders, as well.

It is always heart-wrenching to have to break the news to those families that their loved one has died in a fire. Most people imagine the worst scenarios, not understanding that it is the hot, toxic smoke that kills. Then the fire has its way.

How many times have we found our victims right next to the bed? They stand, take one searing breath and collapse. Or as in one sad case: they almost make it out, fumbling with the lock to the door before succumbing so close to clean air. So many fires, so many lives lost. Every one affected me in some way, some more than others.

One day, driving away from three angelic-looking juveniles I had just interviewed, I called my partner, Charlie, to vent. I explained that the boys had been playing in a garage where they set a fire that burned the grandmother's house down.

I was extremely grateful everyone was okay and that this time I wouldn't be digging an 8-, 7-, and 5-year-old, or grandma, out of the still-smoking rubble. I was extremely pissed at the history of the boys' lives. I was sick and saddened that life was so unfair and so crappy for these boys.

As I railed against the unfairness of angel boys with hopeless futures, of the dysfunction, abuse, and neglect that they had already endured at such young ages, it made the world seem so wrong. My heart ached and my throat burned, I could barely talk. The hopelessness and sad hurt stayed with me. I still think about those boys.

I had taken the training, the "juveniles with fire" course. It was a good course, well-designed by our then educator,

Judy O. Kulich; it was cutting edge. Once the course is completed and a task book worked through, a certificate was given that allows the assessor tools to assess juveniles that are involved in fire behavior.

It is designed to ensure that the proper tools are used to make recommendations for the child involved. It is not designed to make you a social worker or prepare you for what you hear while making those assessments.

Working with the juvenile departments, I gained an understanding and a huge respect of what those folks have to deal with on a daily basis.

I dealt with the loss of peoples' lives in my job. I was also dealing with loss at home. The distance and lack of common ground between Ben and myself grew. I loved music; he loved motorcycles. I wanted to camp, he was more inclined for a motorcycle run. All valid ways, just different.

I wondered how life might be on my own, and how life might be for Ben with a woman who loved to ride as much as he did. He hated change, and I embraced it. I believed the only thing in life you truly can count on is change, nothing stays exactly the same. To me, change was a growth of spirit.

I wanted a different house with property, and Ben thought I wanted too much. It felt a little like when I got my braces at almost 40–did I really need them at this age? No, but I wanted them! As a poor child, I could never afford them and, dang it, I had wanted straight teeth all my life!

Now the need to *be* me, and *know* me, grew. I grappled with the decision to leave my marriage. I could limp along and keep everyone else happy, keep status quo, keep things as they were, and not disappoint my family . . . couldn't I? It was years of agonizing, feeling like there was something I needed to do for me. In the end, I came to the decision that we are all responsible for our own happiness.

After 30 years, our time together came to an end. Ben let me go. I left him the house he loved so much, trying not to disrupt his life completely. It was sad, heartbreaking, and sometimes I wish I would have stayed. Only sometimes.

Chapter 19

Oh, I think a change would do you good
Oh, I think a change would do you good
Oh, a change would do you good
– Sheryl Crow

Most people avoid change if possible. It can bring about myriad emotions, such as loss of control, feelings concerning competency, can I do this? There is always a ripple effect of those involved directly and indirectly. I experienced all this and more as I began letting family and colleagues know of our change.

I had never lived on my own. I had gone from my childhood home to managing as a married adult and a mother, skipping all the steps in between. It was like going back in time.

It was a perfect solution for me when my good friend, Dawn, let me rent her small mother-in-law cottage. In the past, I had loved visiting her property, which I referred to as "a little bit of heaven."

It was five acres of green abundance with fruit trees, garden, and wildlife. It was because of this abundance that I referred to Dawn as "one of the richest women" I knew. It would be a healing place, and I wouldn't be completely alone, sharing dinners and great times. With my sister helping me move and my dad hauling furniture, I felt like a kid on my own for the first time.

It became a time of reinventing myself. I settled into a new life on my own. Due to changes and the absence of our deputy in Roseburg, work was crazy. We concentrated on addressing the most immediate priorities.

Minor duties and meetings fell by the wayside. Time flew by with the hectic schedule. I would plan to drive to Roseburg for a juvenile fire assessment, pick up plan reviews, get a few required inspections done, then a call would come in or a request for a fire investigation derailed all the plans. It was like putting out spot fires.

I got the call for the Sutherlin fire while on another fire scene in Lake Creek. Arson detectives Russ Jones and Tom Hatch were on scene. The 911 call was from a male who stated his son broke into his home and tried to kill him. The eyewitness had his throat slashed, so he would not be able to help us understand exactly what happened until much later.

Upon arrival, the ambulance crew called for fire response as there were items on fire in the driveway, and the house was on fire. This was clearly arson based on the 911 report. The arson detectives were in charge, and I would assist with determining the fire's origin.

A walk around revealed the house was mostly intact with one back bedroom burned significantly. Following contamination protocols, we washed our tools and boots, and entered.

Working our way through the house, we photographed and documented the fire patterns, all indicating the fire moved from the bedroom. Finally, we were at the room of origin. Very slowly, very carefully, we cleaned away debris examining every detail.

We located a female body and began brushing debris gently from her head and face . . . . Where was her face? Confused, I checked her position, yes, she was oriented lying on her back. Oh damn! Her face was covered with tape. Duct tape was wound around and around. No one deserved this kind of death.

Seven hours after we found the body of a much-loved community educator, police arrested the couple's son for murder, attempted murder, and arson. The good work of detectives diligently tracking down the evidence resulted in a cooperative effort with officials retrieving him off a plane in Palm Springs when it landed, after his effort to flee.

Which office to go to today? I was making my plan for the week. Roseburg state police had just built a new patrol office, perched above I-5 on the north side of town. I had orders to occupy it enough to keep dibs on it. Already our new arson detective located there was eyeballing it.

The process to fill deputy positions was postponed again. Charlie and I were covering the south, with me occupying the Klamath office, and my office in Jackson

County, Roseburg, and Coos Bay, while those in charge drew new district lines and set up hiring processes. New management, new deputies, change, it all took time.

In the meantime, we scrambled in react mode to the highest priority requests. A fire would always take highest priority. It was like a being a ball in a ping pong game: here, there, everywhere. Sutherland has a fire; now go to Klamath, they had a fatality; mandatory meetings in Salem. I put thousands of miles on the state truck.

One day, I had a handful of required inspections in my hand and headed out of the Central Point office to drive to Klamath. As I began to shut down my computer, I saw a message from a fellow state worker, Kevin Johnson. Kevin was the brother of my singing/playing partner Ken Johnson. Ken was a recently retired fire marshal who, with his wife, recently moved out of the valley.

For years, Ken and I had played music wherever we could. Ken was a mentor, friend, and colleague. In years past, we had even played for his family at their annual camp. It was at that camp where I met his younger brother, Kevin.

Funny and always smiling, everyone loved Kevin. I can remember how I thought he and his wife made such a cute couple, so fun and happy. They seemed to enjoy each other. Over the years, I had seen them a few times and wondered how would it be to have a marriage like that? Lucky them.

Here it was a few years later, as I sat talking with Kevin at a restaurant in Klamath, he asked how I was doing after being married so long and now on my own? Was it worth leaving, was I happy? Having such a great listener, I went on and on about how it was hard, but I didn't regret anything; in fact, I had a goal of going on a bona fide date, since I had never really had one. A goal for my 50th birthday!

At this time, I was also working on getting into the life coaching business, so I went on telling Kevin enthusiastically about my plans until I noticed he was looking quite sober.

Oh, crap, I thought, as he revealed he wasn't happy in his marriage. He explained he was thinking of leaving his wife. Would my life coaching help him? I began to back-pedal quickly, "You should work to make it good, leaving is not a good option . . . " Uh oh! Creator, what is this about?

That meeting in Klamath changed the course of our lives. It was a head-scratching time for me. I believe all things happen for a reason, but I was having a hard time figuring out this sudden strange turn of events. He did end his marriage–in record time.

He would be the one to show up to meet my family with flowers and best intentions. He would become my gift from the Creator; he became my husband.

I have come to realize that the Creator knows what the plan is. Now I just give thanks every day that I opened myself to this wonderful gift who is my best friend, confidant, my gift from God, my sweet husband, Kevin Ray Johnson.

Who knew? The second part of my life is that question over and over. Who knew life could be so good? I knew I had been loved, but I had never in my life been loved, cherished, and adored like this. Who knew that life could be easy and fun most of the time?!

Who knew such a sweet spirit would come for me? Who knew love would come, the beautiful property would come, and contentment would come with it? Who knew, I, lover of the ocean all my life, would come to be married by a captain on a private island in St. John?

We began our lives together purchasing a small house on a beautiful piece of land with a creek running through it. Now when the phone would ring, my husband would be helping me get out the door. With coffee, snacks, and a smile, he would send me on my way. My personal life grew better and better, work grew more stressful.

Over the years, I had my methods of dealing with fire, death, and the stress: Call my partner, Charlie, or Krissy, to vent and cry; embrace my Native teachings of smudging and prayer; visit the native healer for some doctoring, get some exercise preferably outside in nature, and stuff the pain of it somewhere deep inside.

The stress was taking its toll. I had inflammation issues, achy joints, itchy spots, and alopecia–unexplained hair loss. Doctor visits brought limited relief. All this was lumped into the heading of "auto immune disease," made worse by stress.

I made attempts to eliminate this and that, visualizing health and well-being, riding a health roller coaster. It all came to a head in March of 2015. Of all the deaths I had been a witness to, it was the Brookings fire that really hurt me. Not all at once, but a little at a time.

Chapter 20

I don't know how it started,
Can't seem to make it stop
It's got the best of me
Guess I gave it a head start
Once you let it in
Can't seem to get it out
The ragged blues will get you
If you don't watch out
–"Ragged Blues," Cindy DeGroft

When answering the phone in the middle of the night, it is always difficult to hear, "It's a fatality." And what is worse to hear is, "We have three bodies." As I sat up, grabbing my pen and paper, I began running through the checklist in my mind with dozens of questions to ask.

En route to Brookings, while talking with fire command, I got the update: two of the children made it out. Grandma, Grandpa, and a 4-year-old are inside. I steeled myself, this is going to be a rough one.

Arriving on scene, I was met with the image of weary, wet firefighters with dirty faces wearing sad expressions that seem to say, "We didn't make it in time." It made me remember my first fatal fire, knowing there is a body in there that was not saved, and expecting to see the well-known ravages of fire.

Initially, they were unsure if the mother of the children was inside, as well. Upon my arrival, I found she was out of the house; they tracked her down. She was on her way to the burn center with the 1-year-old.

As I walked down the drive, I saw the remains of the trailer. I caught my breath; I had lived in a trailer just like it. Small, built to burn with coated wood interior and very small, narrow windows in the rear.

I can remember after becoming a firefighter, educating people about fire safety and how imperative it is to have two ways out. I had often thought of that trailer I had lived in with my babies. How dangerous it had been! Single-wide crammed with living, not conducive to escape; it even had a small wood-burning stove!

It is amazing how you really don't think about it until fire affects your life. I had considered us very lucky in retrospect. Thank goodness, we never had a fire. How could anyone ever escape out those metal half windows?

Here I stood, looking at those very half windows. I could imagine how a small 1-year-old could be pushed though it in an emergency, but how did the older child fit through?

Thinking about the chain of events, I kept my mind on the sequence of events and not the image of babies being crammed through half windows as heat and smoke filled the tiny house. There would be no way to keep the images out of my mind that waited just inside the window.

We would have to cut the wall away at the window to gain access to process and remove the bodies. The cuts were made and the metal wall peeled back. The blackened room filled with light.

Grandpa had collapsed away from the window backward onto a bed. His body was burned and blackened, but intact. Grandma had fallen from where it looked like she had been on the dresser getting the kids out.

We were cleaning the debris and moved her body before seeing the small form behind her on the floor. Trying to keep the running commentary quiet in my head that wanted to compare this small child to my granddaughter, I photographed and mapped out the position of the bodies. She was our granddaughters age; she was her size.

As we worked, we wondered why they couldn't escape. The rear door was near the small back bedroom. Did the grandparents come to the children only to be held back by smoke unable to exit the back door? I would not let my mind think about the grandparents.

Being a grandparent was one of the most cherished roles in my life. We had loved and protected our grandkids, and we would gladly die to save any one of them. It was way too hurtful to think about. I made myself focus on the task at hand.

Later, after processing the fire, we determined that a heater had been too close to combustibles, igniting in the living room area. As I left the fire, I tried to digest the horror of children and grandparents dying in such a senseless, tragic way.

I worried about the firefighters. For some, this was the first fatal fire they had responded to. Any first fatal fire encounter must be mentally digested, but this fatal fire was especially hard on those who lived and worked in this community. These selfless volunteers had kids this age, kids who went to school with these children.

The chief was seeing to their needs, calling them all together for a process called a debriefing. In the debrief, they would talk out the call, discuss feelings, and offer support. I remember thinking, "Just don't think about it, just don't dwell on it, try to forget." And I tried. I almost never thought about it–for a while.

I was doing my last set of sit-ups when I felt my back wrench. That's how it started. Soon pain, misery, and self-pity surrounded me like a cloud. My back was in pain, I was having crazy, emotional swings, and then I began thinking and dreaming of the Brookings fire. Why that fire? I know now why it was that particular fire. It was so close to home, close to my heart.

In retrospect, I see a picture of myself in my mind's eye. Arms outstretched, concentrating hard, balancing plates – plates full of stuff. And while the sailing was fairly smooth, I could do a million things, and be all things. The pain in my back made me feel weak and pitiful. I couldn't keep all the plates in the air balanced, something had to crash to the ground.

I was off work, I was feeling horrible, and now I was not

sleeping. I began having nightmares that left me feeling off balance from a lack of sleep. Flashbacks of the scene began to pop into my head unannounced. After battling this depressed, painful state as long as I could, I turned to our employee assistance program.

The Employee Assistance Program (EAP) offers free, confidential services designed to help employees prevent or resolve personal, family, and workplace problems affecting that employee's well-being and job performance. I was relieved that I finally sought professional help.

What is it in us that makes us feel we are being weak to ask for help? I was feeling very puny and weak! I figured I just better admit it and get some help. I was diagnosed with post-traumatic stress disorder (PTSD).

In fairly quick order I began feeling much better. My back healed as I worked with a process called eye movement desensitization and reprocessing (EMDR), a fairly new, nontraditional type of psychotherapy. It's growing in popularity, particularly for treating post-traumatic stress disorder. The flashbacks and nightmares retreated, and I began feeling like me again.

Throughout this, my husband supported me, encouraged me to get help, and ultimately introduced the concept of retirement.

In the past when other deputies and fire marshals would talk about retirement, my eyes would glaze over, that would never apply to me! Starting my career so late in my life, I always imagined I would work until one day I would just fall over, die, and that would be the end of my career.

It was my husband who introduced the fact that, despite my late start in my career, as a police and fire employee I could actually retire at 55.

Recognizing that police officers and firefighters face high risks, high stress, and often have shorter careers, state law allows them to retire sooner than general service workers.

It was a very interesting concept at the time, one I had never considered. It is one I have come to believe is a wise practice.

Emergency personnel deal with some of the most devastating, mind-boggling scenes imaginable. As a responder, you learn to deal with it. I had up to that point done just that . . . dealt with it.

Of the hundreds of hours of training I had received over the years, I don't ever remember having any serious training on nutrition, signs of depression, and the real effects of stress. Even retirement at 55 seems a terrible sentence for those who do carry the weight of such high-level stress occupations, especially fire deaths. I was happy for what the department offered by way of assistance, so once again I moved forward.

Living small had allowed us to pay off the gorgeous property we had found to live and garden on. With no real debt, I could retire if I wanted to. I had worked hard my whole life, which was exactly why my husband voted for retirement.

I had never thought of it, but now I was thinking hard. It was almost impossible after a life time of work to imagine not having a job. I had defined myself by what I could do and accomplish, what and who would I be if I didn't have a title and job to go to each day?

At this time, I spotted an employment advertisement in the Daily Dispatch, a trade website for the fire service.

I saw that my alma mater, Jackson County FD3, was looking for a person to fill a prevention position in Fire and Life Safety. Giving back to the community, focusing on serving a smaller area (less driving), working more with the local kids and community, was appealing. Not to mention that the district Prevention Specialist made more money than I did with half the responsibility!

I was intrigued. To spend the rest of my fire service career working at the department where I had gained my experience and served so long as a volunteer firefighter appealed to me. It would be a step back from my current position, but it would allow me to concentrate all the skills and knowledge I had in prevention and education.

As the workload and effect of covering multiple districts increased every year, and the responsibilities also increased, I concluded that concentrating on a predefined area could be a good thing! I decided that I would apply. I would give it over the creator to lead me. If I was meant to work several more years, this would happen; if I did not get the position, I would retire. Either way I would win.

Chapter 21

Through many dangers, toils, and snares,
We have already come
'Twas grace hath brought
Us safe thus far
And grace will lead us home . . .
–"Amazing Grace," Christian hymn, John Newton, 1779

"Ammaaazzzzing grace . . . " The words of the song reached through the wall into my office. "Hey, is that Gaylon singing!?" Pushing away from my desk, I went to investigate. My office adjoined the training room at the State Police office. On training days, through the wall we could hear the grunts and laughs of the hard work the troops put in to stay in top physical shape.

Gaylon Couch was the lead trainer and a specialized bomb technician for OSP. He was also the arson investigator that had filled the open position in our office. Affectionally referred to as a "pit bull with lockjaw," I loved his dogged determination chasing down arsonists. He would go to great lengths to search out the truth and catch the responsible party. Knowing he would follow every lead and do everything in his power to help solve the fire, we all loved working with him.

"Hey, keep it down in there!" I admonished him with a smile. Seriously though, I didn't know he sang so beautifully. We were occasionally in Salem at the same time at some of the same training, I always had my guitar, I made him promise we would sing together the next time.

Unfortunately, there would be no next time. In just six short months, Gaylon would be gone. His life cut way too short by an aggressive brain tumor.

This loss was devastating on so many levels. It made me realize life is way too short. It also solidified my resolve to retire should the job position go to another candidate. Inside, I think I hoped it would. The 23 years spent in the fire service had been great, but I had a feeling the Creator wanted more light, love, and happiness for me. If I secured the position in education, I would work some with kids, have less stress, but was that my path now? I would await the results and that would be the answer.

When I received the news that the position had gone to another fine candidate, I was happy. It was for me the answer I was ready for.

Making the decision to leave the Office of the State Fire Marshal was bittersweet, and timely. In 2016, the office was relocated, joining with Oregon State Police in a brand-new building located at 3565 Trelstad Ave. SE, Salem. The era of the Portland Road office was over, and my time as a deputy there, at end.

It was hard to say good-bye to the family that makes up the Office of the State Fire Marshal. It was a hard time in our lives at home, as well.

It became one of the saddest nights of my life when I received a call telling me that that my ex-husband, Ben, was at Rogue Regional Hospital in critical condition. He had crashed his motorcycle, and he had massive head injuries.

We knew he had been having issues with his eyes, problems with bright light. Never wanting to go to a doctor or admit anything is wrong, he hadn't addressed it. Now we wondered just how bad it had been. Of course, he was driving fast, that's how he liked it, high speed with the wind in his hair.

It had been a conflict for me in the past: where is the line between life and death intervention? As an emergency responder, I had witnessed many deaths. Beautiful deaths, such as an elder with paperwork indicating "do not resuscitate." I could almost see his spirit lift gently away. A peaceful transition as his family prayed, and we stood by.

Contrasted by the efforts of trying to revive a body that has already expired, cracking ribs as we attempt to revive, praying the paramedic, a senior responder, will quickly get there to call the death. I understood that in some cases this helps the family see that everything possible was done to save their loved one, but where is the fine line of dignity in death?

In Ben's case, it was like being herded along. There was no question or discussion of whether he would want to be handled this way–he would not.

He had a secret belief he would die in a motorcycle crash, and he believed he would be okay with it. In fact, we had joked about it. If I got eaten by a shark scuba diving, I would die happy doing what I loved; if he died in a crash, he would die doing what he loved.

Here we were. We sat numb, listening to the report of how bad his injury was, watching the animated face of our teller as gory details spilled out of his mouth. I wanted to smack him, this was our loved one, not an exciting case to be expounded on. I was glad my daughter wasn't there yet.

They cut his skull to remove the pressure. They pumped him full of nutrients and us full of hope. They dragged the inevitable on and on.

The medical folks got his body to fight when it was so clear his brain would never recover. He would hate this, and yet there is a very guilty feeling saying those things. Thankfully, we finally had a meeting where it was allowed to be said: they were out of tricks, there was no brain activity, he could be allowed to die.

All those fancy tricks had a price. Now we had to starve him in order for him to make his way to the other side. I watched my daughter suffer day after long day. What is humane about this? For him, for his family, and appointed best girlfriend who sat with him day after day, how humane is this? The doctors said, once they stopped supportive care and feeding it would be days, maybe a week.

Days went by, and then it was weeks. Still they sat with him praying. The doctors were surprised, as they kept saying, "Any day . . . " Ben would leave this world on May 10. I always thought I would be with him when he passed, but I was home recuperating from a scheduled surgery.

I wasn't his wife, but he was my family. He was a dad, grandpa, and friend. We never fought; it wasn't ugly. I always loved him. I always will.

Recovering from surgery had its ups, downs, and setbacks. Still I wanted to have some kind of good-bye ceremony as my retirement approached. In our native tradition, we give back to show our respect and thanks for all we have received. My husband and I planned to provide a good-bye feast of Indian tacos made and served by our family for the Salem home office, arson unit, and friends from the Department of Public Safety and Standards.

I looked forward to thanking all those I had the pleasure of serving with. In modern society, it is more common to receive a gift at retirement, so I'm sure our odd request to join us for Indian tacos was a bit confusing for folks. Sadly, Ben's passing and my own delayed healing caused us to have to cancel the event. I wish I could have said a proper good-bye as my July 1 retirement date quickly approached.

Chapter 22

And when I'm really troubled
And I don't know what to do
Fannie whispers, "Just do your best, we're awful proud of you"

–"Guardian Angels," Naomi Judd

Just like every fire tells a tale, every life tells a tale, as well. In a fire, the tale emerges in the patterns and visible effects that mar objects indicating the path of travel: items devoured, shadows of heat outlining pictures, furniture, bodies–the stories of the ones who survive.

In life, the tale emerges with visible effects as well: what we have done, who are the people we have touched, where is the family we leave behind, the people who love us and who we have loved, the determination of a life well lived or lived by accident?

I think back to the little, poor girl lying in a sunny field eating stolen grapes; the adolescent searching shelves for book titles that include "wisdom," "knowledge," or the like; the young mother playing with her children; the now retired Deputy State Fire Marshal, and I smile. That's me!

At different points of my life, I have lived by accident, lived reactive and scared, and lived according to others' agendas. With some knowledge and wisdom, I now create on purpose, I live a life of giving back. The visible effects of the choices I make show up as the love of an amazing husband, family, friends, and an abundance of good living.

What brought me to a career in the fire service? I always say the Creator led me here–fueled by my own longing to be of assistance, a wish to do and be more, and with a lot of hard work I was able to have an incredible life experience.

What led me to retirement? I believe without a doubt, the Creator, my husband, and a longing to help others succeed in having their own incredible life experiences. It is with all this in mind that I hope other people can learn from my experiences, failures, and accomplishments.

"Well, those times are gone, but the memories live on,
each time we hear an old favorite song . . ."

Sing Me Back—M. Rose Johnson

Epilogue

I always imagined having a desk positioned in a sunny spot, with books and a window looking out onto my beautiful garden. That is exactly where this book was born.

I feel I was moved by Spirit to write it, and it is my greatest hope that whoever is supposed to read it, is inspired – inspired to create the best life with their given gift of imagination, belief, and action.

I firmly believe it is your birthright to be, do, and have every good thing. I would like the reader to know that all you need is a little imagination, hard work, and a lot of determination to be and do, and you will have whatever life you can dream.

Dance for my brother – Miwok group California

Miwok house and acorn granary – Grinding Rock, California

Our future – what will their stories be?

Made in the USA
Columbia, SC
08 October 2022

68711197R00104